ASSET ON THE RUN

A Michael Brewer Suspense Novel

RYAN STEVENSON
and
RICHARD BRANDEIS

ISBN: 978-1540561367

PRINTED IN THE UNITED STATES OF AMERICA

This book is dedicated to the tireless efforts of free men and women around the world who continue to stand watch over humanity and its survival for generations to come.

1

It was an uncharacteristically cool day for early June and I really needed to get my day going. Finals at Georgetown University were in full swing, and during the same time period our soccer team was in training for a regional finals match. Hoya athletics was a big deal at Georgetown, and this year we had a great shot at the National Intramural-Recreational Sports Associations regional title, otherwise known as NISRA. We had a great team this year, and several of my friends on the team already had been spotted by pro-league soccer scouts.

After dragging myself out of bed, I headed to the bathroom for a shower. As I turned to the mirror above the sink, I looked at myself and said, "Good morning, Michael Brewer." Luckily the man in the mirror didn't reply, so I guess I was still mentally sound and ready to meet the rest of the team for an early practice session before classes started.

Life in Georgetown wasn't really anything special. Oh sure, it was a great university town with a lot of high-end real estate, along with Congressmen, Senators and other agency types that lived in the area, which did not impress me, as I had lived here with my parents all my life. Georgetown was a convenient commute to the Pentagon, where both of my parents worked as civilian employees. Mom was a receptionist for a three-star general, and Dad was an attorney who acted as a liaison between the military and Capitol Hill.

My life was fairly regimented, and now in my junior year I pretty much had my heart set on getting into the field of microbiology. Following in Dad's footsteps as an attorney held little interest for me, and my typing skills, unlike my mother's, were abysmal. As an only child, I know this was a disappointment to Dad, but at the same time he felt I should be able to pursue my own interests.

I thought to myself that I'd better get my day going or my teammates would think I had overslept again. Cramming for finals always took a lot out of me, so the nights devoted to studying were usually spent with my best friend, a pot of black coffee.

2

Mom and Dad were already heading to work and I was flying out the front door. I had changed into my soccer uniform, and after getting into my car, all I needed was for it to start, as I kept putting off buying a battery that it desperately needed. Thankfully, the old girl turned over and I was on my way to the soccer field.

It was only a short drive to the stadium, and luckily I found a spot to park the car. I noticed some of the team starting to warm up, stretching, while others on the team were jogging around the perimeter of the soccer field. Coach Jefferies had just arrived and no sooner had he walked onto the field than he blew his whistle and waved the players toward the center of the field.

There was no doubt there was a lot of Hoya pride on the line this year, as we were only one game away from nailing the regional championship. This would be our final practice before the big game in three days. After a last minute pep talk, the coach split our team in two, and asked one of the backup players to stand in as the other goalkeeper.

My position was a midfielder, and we had some of the most powerful kickers I had ever played with. One of my strongest points was that I could run like the wind. I had earned the nickname of *The Fly*, because I would make these incredible saves, literally flying through the air to prevent a ball from entering the goal.

Paul Litchfield, one of my best friends on the team, was now setting up for a goal. Considering my ability to grab balls on the fly, I was primed to snatch it. All I had to do was time it perfectly. Once Paul saw his chance, he kicked the ball with incredible force, and it was a well-placed line drive heading for the goal. I thought to myself, *Not this time, Paul.*

As I watched Paul's soccer ball head for the goal I knew I could intercept it. I started my run, not realizing exactly where on the field I was. As I was watching the ball get ever closer, I reached out for it, literally flying through the air—and then it happened! My head went crashing into one of the steel goal posts, and then it was lights out.

Little did I realize what was to come next. I vaguely could hear the coach calling my name, but I just felt as if I was drifting deeper into unconsciousness. After that there wasn't much that I could recall. Not the ride to the hospital, the doctors in the emergency room, or even the CAT scan that was performed. I was basically in a coma for the next three days.

3

After a three-day period, I finally started hearing voices around me. As I began to open my eyes, Mom and Dad were standing next to my bed, along with a nurse and a couple of doctors.

The first words out of my mouth were, "What happened?"

The next thing I remember, one of the doctors introduced himself, and then took out a pen light that was shining in my eyes.

"Michael," the doctor said, "I would like you to follow my finger with your eyes."

"I can do that," I replied.

"Very good, Michael. Your CAT scan showed a small subdural hematoma, and it was touch-and-go as to whether we were going to have to operate to relieve the pressure. At this point it seems to be resolving itself, but I think another CAT scan in a couple of days will give us a better idea, just to make sure."

"You mean I'm going to have to stay here a few more days?" I asked. "I'll miss the big game, Doc. I have to get out of here now!"

"I don't think so, young man. You're not going anywhere, and certainly aren't in any shape to go running around a soccer field."

"Mom, Dad, please talk to these people," I begged. "I can't let the team down this close to the finals."

At that point Dad leaned over my bed and whispered into my ear.

"Michael, there is no way in hell you're leaving this place until the doctors give us the all-clear. From what the doctors have told us, this was a very serious concussion and you're going to have headaches for a while. So just listen to what the experts say, and forget soccer for now, Son."

I was beside myself. I couldn't shake the feeling that I had let all of my team members down. My head was throbbing, and I asked the doctor if this was a normal response.

"Yes, Michael, it's very common to feel that way. What I'd like you to do is get some rest, so I'm going to give you a little something that will allow you to get some sleep."

"But Doc, I've been sleeping for the last three days," I said.

"Michael," Mom chimed in, "just try to relax and we'll be in to see you later this evening."

"Okay, Mom. I promise I'll behave."

At that point Mom and Dad left to get back to work, and after the shot the doctor had pushed into my IV, the room began to spin as I felt myself drifting off into la-la land. I must have slept right through to the next day, as I didn't remember seeing Mom or Dad come back to visit.

4

I had pretty much lost all track of time, but I knew it had to be morning when a nurse brought in a breakfast tray for me and asked how I was doing.

"I'm feeling much better, thank you. What day is it?" I asked.

"Michael, its nine a.m. and its Tuesday. I believe the doctor is making rounds now and should be in to see you soon. He might be able to give you some idea as to when you can finally go home to recuperate."

"Thanks. I really appreciate it. Lying around in bed just isn't my thing," I said.

"Oh look, Michael, here's the doctor now."

"Good morning, Michael. How are we feeling this morning?"

"I think I'm feeling better, but I would really like to try standing up and maybe doing some walking around the floor."

"Michael, that's actually a good sign," the doctor said. "I'm going to order another CAT scan this morning and if it comes back to my satisfaction, I'll contact the Physical Therapy Department and we'll get you up and see how steady you are on your feet."

"Thanks, Doc. I can't tell you how much I appreciate everything all of you have done for me. I just would like to get home as soon as possible."

"Michael, I wouldn't have it any other way," the doctor said, and with that he left to continue his rounds.

Within several minutes I had an orderly helping me to get on a stretcher for a trip to the Radiology Department for another CAT scan. Hopefully all would be well so I could finally get out of here and back in my own bed at home. Mom was a great cook and I had a funny feeling she was whipping up one of her signature apple pies that you could smell a mile away. I could almost smell the cinnamon as I thought about it, and could almost taste the tartness of the apples. Oh please, let this scan come out all right, and Lord, I promise I'll behave.

After the scan was completed it took only about ninety minutes for one of the neurology residents to arrive with the good news. "The doctor looked at the scan and gave the all-clear to get out of bed, but only with assistance," he told me.

"I'll use a cane or crutches if it will get me out of bed any sooner," I told the resident.

"Michael, just wait a few minutes and the physical therapy people will be here to assist you."

It didn't take more than thirty minutes for a well-built and very muscular man to enter my room.

"Good morning, Michael, my name is Gerry. I work in the physical therapy department. You ready to try a little walking?" he asked.

"Sure, Gerry," I said. "What do I have to do?"

"Michael, just sit up in bed first and let your blood pressure stabilize."

"So far, so good, Gerry," I said, after I finally was in a sitting position.

"Great, Michael. Now let's get your legs over the side of the bed. You still with me?" Gerry asked.

"I'm just a little unsteady, Gerry," I said.

"Just sit here for a minute, Michael. I'm going to grab a pair of slippers for you."

Gerry placed a pair of those stretchy non-skid hospital slippers on my feet and then he asked me to grab his arm and stand up.

"How're you feeling, Michael?" he asked.

"Not too shabby, Gerry," I said. "Let's test out these legs."

I was able to walk with help to the nurses' station and back, but there was something going on in my head that I didn't understand. I didn't want to say anything to Gerry for fear that it might increase the length of time I would have to stay hospitalized. This was beyond strange, and I just wanted to get back to bed for a while and try to figure it out.

5

Once I had returned to my room, I thanked Gerry for his help and asked when we might do this again.

"I'll probably be back in about four hours. I have a lot of patients to get to today, Michael," Gerry said.

"Great, Gerry. And thanks again," I replied.

There was no way I was going to let anyone know what had happened during my walk. It honestly scared the crap out of me. When I first had awakened from being in a coma for three days, I noticed a strange buzzing feeling in my head. I just figured I really must have rattled my brain and assumed that things would quiet down in time. Yet, while the buzzing sound seemed to abate somewhat, I noticed something very strange as the physical therapist was helping me walk through the halls.

At first I thought that maybe this bump on the head made me more sensitive to sounds, but it was more than that. As I walked past a patient's room with the door partially open, I could see a patient talking on a phone, and I was able to hear distinctly both sides of the conversation that was taking place.

Then as I passed another patient's room, I saw a doctor facing the patient's window with his cell phone to his ear. I had to be at least thirty feet away from him, yet again I could hear his conversation in my head as clear as day. He was talking to his wife, who wanted to make sure he got out of work on time because they had tickets for a concert at Kennedy Center.

As I sat in my bed, a million thoughts began running through my head. Should I tell anyone about this? Could I get into trouble if I heard something that was illegal and then not report it. It was probably too premature for me to take this any further unless I could somehow determine if this was going to be a permanent change or just some passing medical aberration.

What I needed was more time to determine if this was just a fluke, or whether this newfound ability was going to haunt me for the rest of my life. I needed to place myself in certain situations where I actually could do a study to flesh out what was happening. Whatever was happening to me was surely out of the ordinary, and at least I would have the opportunity to test myself again when Gerry came back to help me do a little more walking around the floor. The one thing I did notice was that I had to face in the direction of the person talking on a phone in order to hear, even though that person was too far away for me to hear under normal circumstances.

At this point I really was getting tired and just wanted to sleep for a while, knowing Gerry wouldn't be back for at least four hours. As I began to drift off, I wondered if I could construct a few questions for some of the medical staff, so that in a roundabout way I might find out if this has ever happened to other patients with severe blows to the head. But on second thought, I felt it was best to leave well enough alone until I could prove to myself that this newfound ability was real.

6

The time must have flown by. The next thing I knew Gerry had returned and was gently shaking my shoulder to get me up from my nap.

"Is it that time already?" I asked.

"Yes, it sure is, Michael. Let's get you out of bed and see if we can walk all the way down the hallway and back."

After getting my slippers on, I walked down the hall with Gerry, and as we passed each patient's room I took notice as to whether or not the patient was actively talking on a phone. The first two rooms we had passed didn't even have patients, but then as we approached a solarium where both patients and family could gather to talk, I knew I would get my chance.

I asked Gerry if he could do me a favor and get me a glass of water. He asked if I would be okay and I assured him I would be fine. After he left, I just leaned against a wall that was easily twenty-five feet away from the solarium. As my eyes fixated on people that were talking on their cell phones, I could again make out every single word on both ends of their conversation.

As I scanned the solarium for others that were talking on their phones, it seemed that as long as I looked in an individual's direction, I could totally hear every last word that was spoken. At that moment, Gerry stunned me when he came up from behind me and said, "Hey Michael, here's your water."

"Thanks, Gerry," I said.

"You okay, Michael? You look like you've seen a ghost."

"I guess I'm just a little tired, Gerry. Why don't we go back to the room so I can crawl back into bed."

Gerry walked me back to my room, and as we passed the nurses' station there was a really cute nurse on her cell phone. Even over the background noise, I could hear every word that was said. I knew one young lady that was going to have a hot time after she got off work.

I thanked Gerry for walking me back and suggested, "Maybe we can do this again tomorrow."

"Yes, I should be able to get to you around ten tomorrow morning. So get some rest and we'll get back into it tomorrow."

After Gerry left my room, I knew something had radically changed in my life. How was this possible? I mean, I had read stories about people who had strange things happen to them after an accident, but I apparently had this ability which, at worst, could get me in a whole lot of trouble. On the other hand, I thought of the possibilities and doors this might open if I played my cards right.

This was going to take some real soul searching on my part, but then again, I needed to know if this newfound ability would last, and only time would provide me the answers I was looking for. At least for now, I didn't dare tell anyone about this, not even my parents.

7

It had now been a couple of days since I discovered this new talent I had developed, and finally the day had arrived when I could go home. The last CAT scan showed continued improvement, and apparently the doctors felt it was okay for me to be discharged. The only clothes I had at the time I was admitted was my soccer uniform, so I called my mom and asked her if she could bring me a pair of sweat pants and a sweat shirt, along with a pair of socks and my sneakers.

It was around eleven a.m. when Mom walked into my room. One of the nurses had just gone over my final instructions with me and I was beyond ready to get out of the hospital. My mom was such a gem, and while I was changing and getting ready to leave, she asked me if I had an appetite.

"Are you kidding, Mom? I have a funny feeling you've been doing some baking in my absence."

Mom was a dead giveaway when she smiled and asked if I could smell the apples and cinnamon from my favorite apple pie she had just finished baking and left cooling at home, just waiting for me to dive in.

Once I was finished dressing a male orderly came into the room with a wheelchair and asked if I was ready to go.

"I sure am," I replied. "So let's make tracks to the parking lot. I have an apple pie waiting for me."

With that, Mom smiled, and headed to the elevator with us for a brief trip down to the ground level. The orderly waited with me as Mom went to bring the car around, and after a few minutes he was helping me into the car, and then we were off. I sat in the front passenger seat while Mom drove, as I kept thinking to myself about this new talent I seemed to have developed. It didn't take long for me to understand that this gift was something special. But like many things in life, a situation like this could well be a double-edged sword.

I know Mom was talking and I was giving her short answers—then it happened again. As we passed people on the street that were talking on cell phones, I could hear what they were saying, but with the car moving as fast as it was, one conversation simply bled into another. Finally, as we pulled into our driveway, Mom asked how I was feeling.

"Just a little tired, Mom. I think I'm going to have a slice of that pie you made and then just go up to my room and lie down for a while, if that's okay with you."

"Of course it is, Michael. If there is anything you need, just let me know. I took the day off from work and will be here if you need me," she said.

"Great, Mom, but I think I'll be all right. And that pie does smell so incredibly good."

After I finished my slice of heaven, I went up to my room and threw my soccer uniform into the hamper. Other than the bed in my room, there was a dresser with a flat screen television on top, along with my stereo on shelves just above it. In front of a large bay window sat my really great oak desk that my dad had found on the cheap in a yard sale, which gave me the opportunity to sit and gaze outside. After closing the door to my room, I pulled out my desk chair and sat down, making sure not to look outside. But I had to know if I still had the ability to listen in on conversations, so I couldn't resist peaking out that window, and I had my answer as soon as I lifted my eyes and looked out across the street.

Our neighbors across the street were both military people. I didn't really know them well, although I imagined my parents did, as they traveled in those circles. As I focused on one of the rooms on the second floor of their home, I could hear their phone ringing. A woman picked up and apparently she was told to expect a delivery of a new oven they had purchased. The moment I looked away, the sound stopped. I tried again looking at the same room, and as soon as my eyes were fixed on my target, I again could hear the ongoing call.

This was just too much to take in at the moment, but sooner or later I knew I would have to talk to my parents about this. After hearing a story like this, they probably would think I was crazy. This new ability was now beginning to scare the shit out of me; just thinking of the ramifications was mindboggling.

8

After getting out of the hospital and being home for about five hours, my head started throbbing. I decided just to lie on my bed and close my eyes for a while, and as I was dozing off, I heard my dad come home and start walking up the stairs, probably to see how I was doing. I sat on the side of my bed just waiting for the inevitable knock on my door.

"Mike, it's Dad. Can I come in for a minute? Just wondered how you were feeling."

"Sure, Dad, come on in," I replied.

"How are things going, Son?"

"I can't complain, Dad. It's just that every once in a while I get these throbbing headaches, but I guess that is to be expected after diving head-first into a goal post at school."

"Have you had any other issues, Mike, that the doctor might need to know about? He did say that you would have headaches for some time."

"Dad, I have to be honest with you. There is something else that I just can't put my finger on."

"What do you mean, Son?"

"Dad, I know I received a severe blow to the head, but after getting out of the coma I was in for three days, something really strange took place. At first I thought my head was playing tricks on me. Then I tested myself a couple of times at the hospital and discovered that I have what many would call an amazing talent."

"Now you've piqued my curiosity, Mike. Care to talk about it, Son?"

"Well, Dad, I have this strange ability—I mean, something happened to me and I have this ability to listen in on any private telephone conversations as long as I'm looking in the direction of the person that's talking. That's pretty insane, huh?"

"Mike, do you mean to tell me that ever since you woke up from the coma, you could start hearing these conversations in your head?"

"Yes, Dad, every word. I swear, Dad, if you don't believe me, let's do a little experiment if you're up to it."

"If I'm up to it! Are you kidding me? Let's try a little test. I'm going to go out to my car and sit in it with the door closed and I'm going to make a call to someone on my cell phone. Now is there anything that you have to do to make this work?"

"Dad, all I have to do is look in your direction and I should be able to hear everything you say."

"Okay, Mike, I'm heading to the car right now. Just watch me out the window and after you see me close the door, I'll make the call."

With that, Dad left my room and headed to the driveway. I watched him pull out his cell phone and then get into his car and close the door. I then could see him dialing someone, and I began timing him with a stopwatch I had. The call lasted for roughly three-and-a-half minutes, then I saw him get out of the car and head back to my room. I knew

I was going to get the third degree. After all, Dad was a lawyer.

"Okay, Mike. Did you see me talking on the phone?'

"Yes, Dad, I did."

"Do you have any idea who I called and what was said?"

"Yes, Dad, I do. You called Grandma in California. You first asked her how she was feeling and then she asked how I was doing. She asked you if you thought it might be a good idea to let me travel out to see her. Then you said we should let me just rest for a while, that I just had gotten out of the hospital. Then Grandma said she may just get on a plane to come and see me and you said to her: "There's no rush. Let him rest a few days."

Grandma then said, "You're such a killjoy, James," and laughed. At that point you said you had to run, and here you are. So did I get it, Dad?"

At that point my dad turned as white as a sheet and had to sit down. If he hadn't closed his mouth when he did, his jaw would already have been on the floor. He looked at me in the strangest of ways and yet couldn't utter a word.

"I guess you're impressed, huh Dad?"

"I can't believe that you were able to hear every last word that was spoken, Mike. It's impossible. This has to be some kind of trick you're playing on your old man."

"No, Dad. I don't know what happened to me after the accident, but I now have this incredible ability."

"Mike, incredible isn't the word for it. Listen, Mike, don't speak a word of this to your mother yet. If it's okay with you, I want the two of us to go for a ride when you're up to it and let's put this new ability to a real test."

"Sure, Dad. When would you like to take that ride?"

"Well, today is Thursday. If you feel like it, how about this Saturday?"

"Sure, Dad. That works. I mean it's not like I have anything important I need to do other than rest at this point."

"Mike, just remember—not a word to your mother about this."

With that, Dad gave me a hug and went back downstairs to clean up before dinner. I guess I had let the cat out of the bag and really had no idea where this new ability might take me, but that little voice we all have within us told me that my life would never be the same again.

A million thoughts were racing through my mind. I knew that this new ability or gift, as some might call it, could be used for both good as well as evil. What would happen if this was used in ways that could hurt others, I wondered. There was just way too much to consider, but I was willing at least to go for the ride Dad spoke about, and then take things from there. I also knew I couldn't tell any of my friends about this, nor would I want to. All I could do was think about how paralyzing an ability like this could be if not used for the best of intentions.

9

It was no more than a couple of hours after Dad got home that Mom called up to me and said dinner was ready. As I headed downstairs, each step was excruciating, as the throbbing in my head was getting the better of me.

"Mom, did you happen to pick up the pain killers at the pharmacy?" I asked.

"Yes, Mike. They're right over there by the breadbox on the counter. Still have those throbbing headaches, dear?"

"Yes, Mom, but I know the doctor said they were to be expected for several days."

As we sat down to dinner, I looked toward Dad and he seemed to have regained his composure. He and Mom got into some small talk about a couple that they knew who had been in a terrible car accident, and then the topic turned toward me.

"Mike," Mom asked, "when do you have to get in touch with your guidance counselors at Georgetown to find out about making up your finals for the semester?"

"I was going to do it tomorrow, Mom. I just wanted to rest for a day after getting out of the hospital before trying to get back into the swing of things," I replied.

"Lois, for God's sake, you just brought him home from the hospital. I think we can give our son at least 24 hours and maybe even the weekend before we start mainstreaming him back into any type of schedule. Don't you think so, dear?"

"Why, of course, James. I just didn't want Mike to let school slip. He still has to complete his finals, you know."

"Mom, don't worry about it. I'll talk to school tomorrow and get it all straightened out," I said.

Usually after dinner, Mom and Dad would retire to the living room and watch some of their favorite shows, but this evening Dad just went for some soothing music after a long day at the Pentagon, while Mom caught up with a book she was reading. I poked my head into the living room and told my parents I was just going to make it an early night. The two pills I had taken took care of the headache, and as long as my head wasn't pounding, I was going to try and get some sleep. It had been a long day and I was beat. I got undressed and into a pair of sweat pants and a tee shirt.

Just as I was ready to doze off, my phone rang. It was my best friend in the world and fellow soccer team member, Paul Litchfield.

"Hey, Buddy, got a few minutes to talk to an old friend, or should I call back another time?"

"Hey, Paul, how the hell are you? I'm really sorry I screwed up so bad during practice. It was the last thing I ever expected to happen."

"Man, Mike, you all had us scared shitless. We thought we had lost you forever, and the sound your head made when you hit that pole sent chills down my spine. I knew that moment that something really bad had just happened."

"Well, Paul, it was bad enough to keep me in the hospital for several days, but things are slowly returning to normal."

"That's so great to hear, Mike. Maybe if you're up to it, we can get together over the weekend. How does that sound?"

"Paul, I do have some plans with my dad for Saturday, but if Sunday works for you and we can keep things low key, that would work," I said.

"Mike, tell you what; I'll give you a call Saturday evening around eight, and maybe we can go out and get some lunch on Sunday, my treat."

"Sounds good to me, Paul. I'll be looking forward to it. I also have to give the university a call tomorrow and find out what I have to do to take my finals."

"That shouldn't be a problem, Mike. If you want, I can talk to your guidance counselor and just tell them to expect a call from you, if that's okay."

"Sure, Paul. I probably won't be calling in until at least ten tomorrow morning, so if you can talk to Mrs. Hudson, I would really appreciate it. Just don't go overboard like you usually do, making it sound like I was on my death bed, okay?"

Paul, who had a great sense of humor, broke out laughing. But as friends go, you couldn't ask for anyone who was as nice as Paul. He was just a great guy to have as a friend. Although in the back of my mind, until my dad and I could get to the bottom of my newfound ability, I didn't dare mention this to anyone, not even to Paul.

"Listen, Paul, I took a couple of pain killers and they're making me really drowsy, so if it's okay with you, can we cut this a little short? I really need to get some sleep."

"Not a problem, Mike. Have a good night and we'll talk tomorrow. I'll also let the rest of the team and the coaches know you're just about back to normal."

"Well, Paul, I wouldn't exactly call it normal, but close enough. Have a good night, Paul, and we'll talk soon."

The time seemed to be passing quickly and if I were going to take advantage of feeling drowsy, now was the time to call it a day.

10

The next morning, for the first time in the last week, I woke up without a headache. So far, so good; I knew I had to take things easy, so after getting up I just took a shower, got dressed and headed downstairs for breakfast. Mom had decided to take today off as well, and at least we were able to catch up on things while she kept an eye on me just in case I ran into a problem.

After breakfast, I told Mom I would be on the phone with Georgetown so that I could arrange taking my finals. I helped her with the dishes and it actually felt good being able to move around without those damned headaches. I headed back to my room and decided to close the curtains, because every time I looked in any direction, if someone was on a phone, I heard their conversation. So I figured this was at least the easiest way to prevent hearing anything other than the individual I was talking to.

Calling the university was always an experience that I wouldn't wish on anyone. After getting through a maze of endless prompts, I finally was able to get my guidance counselor, Mrs. Hudson, on the line. Thankfully, Paul had come through for me and had stopped in to tell her I would be getting in touch. At least that expedited the process, because by the time I had reached her, she already had a schedule set for me as to when I could take my finals.

At least that was out of the way. After I finished my call, I heard Mom walking up the stairs, and I knew what was ahead for me. When she passed my room, she looked somewhat confused as to why I had my curtains closed.

"Mom, I close them because the sunlight does bother me a little. Maybe keeping them closed is helping with the headaches, because right now, I don't have one."

"Okay, Mike. I just wondered why they were closed. I have to run out to get some food-shopping done. Do you think you'll be okay while I'm gone?" she asked.

"Mom, I'll be fine, but if something does come up, I promise I will call you immediately, okay?"

"Sure, Mike. I'll be leaving in just a few minutes."

I was kind of relieved that Mom would be out of the house, as there was something I wanted to try while she wasn't around. After she left for the market, I went into my parents' bedroom and found a pair of binoculars that I knew was on a shelf in my dad's closet. I had so many questions about this newfound ability, and I wondered if I could still hear calls while looking through them. Could the lens elements possibly restrict my ability, or did it make any difference at all?

I grabbed Dad's binoculars and went back to my room and opened the curtains. I picked out a commercial building in the distance that had to be more than five miles away. I focused in on the tenth floor. It was a corner office and I noticed a man sitting behind his desk, but he wasn't on the phone. Then I looked at a higher floor and I did find a woman talking on a cell phone. As soon as I brought the image into focus, I could hear every word of her conversation. At that point, the hairs on the back of my neck stood up. How in the world was this possible?

I tried several other buildings and consistently got the same result. I placed Dad's binoculars back in their case and returned them to the shelf in his closet. I was tempted to give Dad a call at his office in the Pentagon, but considering how the government has gotten into the habit of listening to phone calls, I figured it was better just to wait until he got home. I had a feeling that after talking to my father, he would want to test me himself on Saturday.

Mom probably would be home soon, so I decided just to kill time and try the internet to see what information I could find. I wondered if there had been any cases like this reported in the medical field. I knew there were confirmed stories about people that did spontaneously combust. They just caught fire with no external heat source. But how many people took a hit to the head and started hearing telephone conversations?

I probably had spent hours looking for any indication that this had ever happened to anyone else. If it did, there was literally no record of it anywhere I could find. I sat back in my desk chair with my arms clasped behind my neck and thought, *you lucky devil.*

11

It wasn't long after my search for medical oddities was over that I heard Mom arrive back home. I felt good enough to want to help her with her packages, but when I got to the car she insisted I just take it easy, saying she could manage.

"I hope you don't mind my sneaking another piece of that fantabulous apple pie you made, Mom."

"Why would I mind, Mike? After all, I made it especially for you?"

"Then you won't be mad that I actually had two slices," I joked.

"You're too much, Michael. How would you like to help me get dinner ready? You know how your dad likes to have it ready the moment he walks into the house."

"Sure, Mom. Just tell me what you would like me to do."

"How about chopping up those scallions, and could you break up that block of cheddar into small pieces, Mike?" Mom asked.

Mom was going to make one of her signature dishes. She made a really incredible *Veal Marsala*, with fresh mushrooms, along with sautéed French green beans as a side. Then she would create these amazing baked potatoes loaded with melted cheddar, bacon, and scallions. It was an impressive meal to behold, and I know my dad, after a week of work, really appreciated coming home to a great meal.

It was nearly five in the evening when I heard Dad pull into the driveway. I kind of felt like an excited kid getting ready to go to his first prom, and I couldn't wait to tell dad about what I had tried with his binoculars. I had a feeling it would blow his mind altogether.

Dad looked pretty exhausted as he walked in the front door.

"Hard week, Dad?" I asked.

"Yep. Between worrying about you and problems at work, I'm pretty beat, Mike."

I followed Dad into his bedroom and waited for him to get washed up for dinner. Once he dried his hands, I had to tell him what happened today, without Mom knowing.

"Dad, can we talk for a moment before dinner?" I asked.

"Sure, Mike. How are you feeling today?"

"Dad, I feel pretty good, and didn't even have a headache today."

"Great, Mike. So what's on your mind?"

"Dad, I borrowed your binoculars today and brought them into my room. I was looking at a building that had to be at least five miles away, and after I focused on a woman in her office on her phone, I could hear the conversation as if I were on the other end of the line."

"Mike, are you serious?"

"Yes, Dad. Dead serious."

"Mike, we're going to take a drive into DC tomorrow and try a little experiment. If what you say is true—and I have no reason to believe otherwise—I think we should both see a specialist that may be able to help us."

"A specialist, Dad?" I asked.

"Mike, he's a psychiatrist and an old collage friend that I totally trust. Maybe we can get some answers from him as to what is going on and whether this is a temporary or permanent condition."

"Dad, that sounds great because I was looking on the internet today, and I couldn't find any similar events that had taken place."

"Mike, let's talk about this when we're in the car tomorrow for our drive, and at this early stage, still not a word to your mother about this, okay?"

"Sure, Dad. Not a problem. Let's go eat. Mom made your favorite and I'm starving."

12

As we sat down to dinner, Mom and Dad were in their small-talk routine. Since I seemed to be feeling better and without headaches, that was one concern they didn't have to worry about at the moment, but what I was getting somewhat concerned about was my dad's idea of seeing a psychiatrist. If this ability I had ever became known, I wondered what position this would place me in. Would my current life course change?

I had so many questions that were running through my mind, but rather than get stressed over it, I figured Dad would keep things under control and there would be little to worry about. How I wish I had a crystal ball at the moment. The best I could do was just to let my life play out as it would, and then deal with anything that came my way as it arose.

After we finished dinner, both Dad and I helped Mom clean up, and then I retired to my room to get some studying done for my upcoming finals that Mrs. Hudson had arranged for me to take. I figured Dad would stay downstairs with Mom, but after half an hour, I heard him walking upstairs. It wasn't long before he entered my room with his binoculars in hand.

"Hey, Mike," Dad began, "I grabbed the binoculars and wondered if you could give me a demonstration of your unique ability. I'm just trying to understand this, so that I might be able to begin explaining to the doctor I'd like you to see."

"Sure, Dad. Is there any particular place you would like me to home in on?" I asked.

"Son, try the neighbors across the street like you did earlier," Dad suggested.

He handed me the binoculars and I focused them on the neighbors' living room where I could see a man and a woman seated.

"Anything yet, Mike?" Dad asked.

"No, Dad, nothing yet; neither of them is on the phone at the moment. I can't read minds, only hear phone conversations," I smiled. "Oh, wait a minute. The phone must be ringing, because the man in the room just picked up."

"Are you hearing anything yet?" Dad asked.

"Yes, Dad. I am. I really don't know the neighbors, but is the man in the military?" I asked.

"Yes, he is, Mike. I see him on occasion at different Pentagon meetings. What is the conversation about, Mike?" Dad asked.

"Dad, he's talking to a man he's addressing as General Morrison, and they're talking about a military exercise that is scheduled to take place off the Georgia coast. It's supposed to take place in two weeks. They're both talking about the movement of troops using the I-95 corridor."

"Mike, that's enough for now," Dad said. "I'm convinced of your ability, but there is one more test I would like for us to do tomorrow, if that's okay with you."

"Sure, Dad, no problem. Can I ask you a question?"

"Yes, Son, what is it?"

"Were you aware of this military exercise that is being planned in two weeks?"

"Yes, Mike, I know all about it. We'll get back into this tomorrow when we take our drive. It's been a long week for me and I told your mother I was going to turn in early."

"Sure, Dad. Here, take your binoculars back."

With that, my dad left my room, but I noticed he had this really strange look of concern on his face. I had just chalked it up to his being tired, but my gut was telling me there was something more to his apprehension, and I wanted him to open up a bit more and let me in on it.

At this point I was really getting tired, so I decided to get changed and ready for bed. At least I had proven one more thing to myself this evening. While I was peering across the street listening in, it had begun to rain heavily. Even through a heavy rain, I was still able to hear everything that was being discussed over the phone.

I got into bed and while lying there on my back, I just began to stare at the ceiling, wondering about the what-if's regarding my newfound ability. I was smart enough to know that this was not only some fabulous gift, but that there was a darker side to it as well. Could I be placing my own life in jeopardy? Could that be why my dad had that strange look on his face? I guess only time would tell, but given my character, I knew I would resolve to use this ability only to help others in some way. Just how remained to be seen, yet I was willing to see where things progressed from here.

13

I had an unusually restless night, and if I even got a few hours' sleep, that was more than it felt like. I knew today would be interesting—I just didn't know how interesting yet. I jumped into the shower and the last thing I missed were those headaches I was having. Hopefully they were gone for good. After drying off, I got dressed and headed downstairs for breakfast.

"Morning, Mom. Where's Dad? Still sleeping?" I asked.

"No, Mike. He said he wanted to gas up the car and that you and he were going to take a drive. He said he had some paper work to pick up at his office and thought you might like to get out of the house for a while."

"Cool, Mom; that sounds like a great idea."

As I was finishing breakfast, I heard Dad pull into the driveway.

"Good morning, Mike," Dad said. "Feel like joining me for a road trip? I have to head into the office and bring some work home."

"Sure, Dad. Count me in."

We helped Mom clean up, then we both gave her a kiss and told her we would be back before she even missed us, and headed for the car. I knew the story line my dad gave to Mom was a head fake, but he must have felt that this trip for some reason was going to be very important. I didn't want to barrage him with a million-and-one questions, so for a while it was just some small talk about school and getting ready to take my finals.

I had noticed that Dad must have sneaked the binoculars out of the house, as they were sitting on the back seat of the car.

We headed east to drive the short distance into DC, and after we found our way to Constitution Avenue, we turned west again and drove slowly down the beautiful boulevard, from where you could see all the monuments and many of the Smithsonian museums. If you never have been to the nation's capital, it truly is a sight to behold. Dad asked me to grab the binoculars in the back seat, which I did. I asked if there was any place in particular he wanted me to scan. He told me just to watch on my right, as he slowed down almost to a crawl. Then I understood what he wanted me to do as the Whitehouse loomed into view. He asked me to zoom in on one of the windows.

"For real, Dad?" I asked.

"Yes, Mike, for real."

I focused in on a series of windows on the ground floor and it didn't take long before I was hearing conversations that were taking place.

"Holy shit, Dad! I've got a conversation going on with a Secret Service agent, and he's talking to someone about making plans for a trip that the President is going to be making to Europe."

"Try another window, Mike," Dad suggested.

I moved my line of sight to the second floor, but couldn't pick up anything.

"Sorry, Dad, but maybe on the weekends the President and his family are up at Camp David," I said.

"That's okay, Mike," Dad replied. "We're going to another building now."

As we continued on Constitution Avenue, Dad pulled within a couple thousand feet of the Federal Reserve building.

"See if you can pick up anything," Dad asked.

I focused in on one of the large windows where I could see someone that was on the phone at the moment.

"Dad, you're not going to believe this, but the man that's currently talking on the phone is making arrangements to transfer several tons of gold bullion from the Federal Reserve Bank of New York to the West Point Depository."

"Good, Mike. Let's move on," Dad said.

We continued on our way, went around the Lincoln Memorial and took the Memorial Bridge across the Potomac, then headed toward the Pentagon. When we were about a mile from the main entrance, Dad asked me to focus on any window where someone may have been talking. It didn't take long for me to connect with a naval officer who was speaking to someone regarding updating nuclear codes for the entire submarine service.

"Dad," I said, hesitantly, "would you like to know when the nuclear codes for all of our submarines are going to be changed?"

"Mike, that's enough," he announced. "I'm totally convinced of your abilities, but we're going to have to talk this over. How about we stop and get a cup of coffee?"

"Sure, Dad. Anything you want is fine with me."

Dad never did pull into the Pentagon, and I figured he had just come up with that story for Mom so she wouldn't catch on to what was happening. I felt sort of like I was keeping something from her about this new ability I had, but I knew that my dad would be able to handle just about any situation that might arise.

As we drove back into Georgetown, we found a little hole-in-the-wall place to sit for a while and just talk. I could tell by the look on my dad's face that he seemed concerned about something, and I knew I was about to find out what that was.

14

After we parked and got out of the car, Dad locked it up, and as we walked toward the restaurant he placed his arm around my shoulders, and said, gravely, "We have to talk."

There was that fatherly, concerned look on his face, and I wasn't sure what was coming next. We entered the restaurant and got a couple of cups of coffee, along with two cheese Danishes, and found a seat in the back of the place. Dad kept looking around, but there wasn't anyone nearby.

"So Dad, what's on your mind?" I asked.

"Mike, neither of us can explain what happened to you, but you have an incredible gift. To have the ability you have can be both a blessing as well as a curse, if you understand what I'm saying."

"I do, Dad. But in a worst case scenario what are you concerned about?" I asked.

"Mike, if word of this ever got out to various agencies, like the CIA or the NSA, I honestly doubt that either your mother or I would ever hear from you again, and the last thing I want for my son is for him to be turned into some experimental lab rat that will never see the light of day."

"Dad, are you serious? I mean, what would organizations like that want with me?"

"Mike, you have such an incredible ability. Just think about it. You could be made to travel to different places in our country or even foreign countries, and be used as a non-traceable spy, and for less than altruistic reasons."

"Gee, Dad, I never gave that any thought. Do you still want me to see this doctor you had mentioned?" I asked.

"Yes, Mike, I do. We need to know if this ability is temporary or permanent, and I know Dr. Stevenson will be able to provide some answers for us. Until we meet with him, not a word of this to your mother. I'll make the arrangements and let you know when we can get in to see him."

"Dad, are you sure you can trust him? I mean this doctor friend of yours?"

"Yes, Mike, I am. I've known Ed for years and we're best of friends. He does a great deal of work currently with the military helping veterans getting over severe PTSD episodes."

"Okay, Dad. I'll take your word for it. Never in a million years did I ever think I would become a microbiologist who would be able to hear individual phone conversations, while potentially being used as a tap on a phone without anyone having to go through the court system to get a court order to do it legally."

Dad gave me one of his unique smiles and said, "We'd better get going or your mother is going to wonder where we've been."

Dad left a couple of bucks on the table for a tip and we headed back to the car for the short ride home. There were a million-and-one thoughts going through my mind and at this point, I didn't know what to expect in meeting this psychiatrist. As long as my dad felt confident in his approach, I had no other choice than to go along for the ride. Oddly enough, of greater importance to me at the moment, was studying for my upcoming finals.

"When we get home, Mike, just play along, and when Mom asks how the trip was, just say it was boring as usual. That I only had to pick up some papers and we weren't there all that long. That it was just nice getting out of the house—something like that. Okay, Mike?"

"Sure, Dad," I replied.

15

Within ten minutes we were back home, and found Mom outside watering the flowers that lined our front porch. Summer wasn't far off and Mom always liked playing in the dirt. On any given day, you could find her pulling weeds or planting different varieties of bulbs that would come up the following spring.

"So how was your outing, boys?" Mom asked.

"Nothing to write home about, Mom, but it sure was nice getting out of the house for a few hours."

"At least you got to see something different, Mike. It was a nice change of pace."

"It was, Mom," I said. "We also drove around DC, and as many times as I've been in D.C. there's always something different to see that I never noticed before."

At that point Dad gave me a stare that could kill. He was probably afraid I might slip, but I winked at him, letting him know I wouldn't breathe a word of what we did in DC. As I continued talking to Mom, Dad opened the back door to the car and removed the binoculars and brought them back into the house. I knew Mom saw that, and when she turned to ask Dad why his expensive binoculars were in the car, he laughed and said he had intended to do some bird watching but never got around to it.

"Your father is such a liar, Mike," she said to me, as we both sheepishly laughed about that comment. You never really know what's going on in the minds of others like your parents, but they sure seemed happily married for the last twenty eight years, and I really hoped that my newfound ability wasn't going to rock the apple cart. The last thing I wanted was to feel guilty about this ability coming between the two of them.

I headed up to my room and saw there was a message from my friend, Paul, so now was as good as any time to call him back.

"Hey, Paul, what's up?" I asked.

"Hey, Mike, how's it going? How are you feeling?"

"Actually, pretty good Paul. I had the chance to get out of the house for a while and finally get some fresh air."

"Say, Mike, they're having a mixer over at one of the offsite frat houses. How about we go and see what kind of trouble we can get into."

"Paul, I really would like that, but I only got out of the hospital a couple of days ago, and I think I'd better just take it easy for a while. Besides, I have to start cramming for my finals. So I'd better stay planted."

"I totally understand, Bud, but you are going to be missed," Paul said.

"I know, but at least say *hi* to all the guys on the team, and tell them while I can't play the final match, I'll be sitting in the stands cheering all of you on, okay?"

"Good deal, Mike. Don't you worry, everyone has been asking for you, and I'm surprised your phone hasn't been ringing off the hook by now."

"I have a feeling my parents were probably fielding calls to the house while I was in the hospital, and they might have told friends and family just to let me get some rest."

"You're probably right, Mike, but I'll let everyone know you're doing much better," Paul said.

"Thanks again, Paul. Don't be a stranger, and if you have some free time tomorrow, why not stop by the house for a while."

"Man, I just might do that, Mike. Just take it easy for now, and you'd better get cracking with those books. Your finals begin next week."

"I will, Paul. Have a great night."

Paul was really a great friend. We had known each other since the third grade, and we were as thick as thieves. We did everything together and I really appreciated the friendship and bond that we had developed over the years.

I didn't realize how fast time was flying by, and as long as I had everything I needed to start studying, now was as good a time as any. I could at least get a few hours in before Mom had dinner on the table.

16

Microbiology may have been a heavy subject for many, but I thrived on learning about life at the microscopic level. At one point I had even given thought to becoming a doctor, but decided that I really didn't want to have to spend a third of my life in training and then start trying to pay back education loans. I just didn't see the value in spending that much time in school. Besides, I really enjoyed lab work and investigative medical research.

Organic chemistry was another area that fascinated me, and my chemistry book was probably as thick as *War and Peace*. I knew most of the information that would probably be on my tests, and I was just glossing over chapters to refresh my memory. It was really strange, but after the hit I took, physical time seemed to be moving faster. It was probably just my imagination playing tricks on me, but I felt it was something to keep an eye on.

It was getting close to dinnertime and the smells coming from the BBQ were making my mouth water. Dad loved grilling, and as long as the weather was cooperating, why not? As a family, we really like to grill foods during the warmer months, and I even remember days when it was pouring rain, and Dad standing outside with an umbrella making sure the steaks didn't turn to charcoal.

I felt pretty comfortable that I knew what I had to in order to pass my finals, so at least for now, I was going to take a break. I could always pick the books up again after dinner. Speaking of which, I might as well get cleaned up and then head downstairs and see if Mom required any help getting ready for the meal.

As I was standing over the sink washing my hands, I think I had one of those out-of-body experiences. I just seemed to zone out as I listened to the water running and watched as it was going down the drain. Its funny how these moments take place, and what pops into your head. All I could think of was my friend, Paul, and the thought that any man that has a friend has the world's richest treasure. There was no question that I had a pretty great life, and with Paul as a friend, I considered myself pretty lucky.

I snapped back from my out-of-body moment when Mom called up and said dinner was nearly ready. I dried my hands and then made my way to the kitchen. Dad was just about ready to pull the steaks off the grill and Mom had made a Caesar salad that was to die for. I grabbed a few napkins and got the table set just in time for Dad to walk in from the back yard with the food. He was very picky in wanting to let the steaks rest before we dived in, and it really did make a difference in letting the juices get reabsorbed, as it enhanced the flavor of the meat.

As we sat down to enjoy the meal, Mom asked if I was doing okay with my studying.

"I think I have it down pat, Mom, but it never hurts to review," I said.

"That's great, Mike," Mom replied. "Have you heard from Paul or any other members of the soccer team?"

"Sure, Mom. I just spoke to Paul a little earlier and he and the team were going out tonight, but I told him I was going to pass since I had been out of the hospital for only a couple of days. Besides, I wanted to study before finals next week."

"Smart move, Mike," Mom said.

Dad was unusually quiet, and I figured he had a lot on his mind. Little did I know until after dinner that he already had spoken to Dr. Stevenson and had set up an appointment for Sunday, of all times. But I guess he felt it was really important to get to the bottom of this.

We finished dinner and I helped Mom get the dishes in the washer and then headed back to my room to study a little more. It wasn't long before Dad entered my room and told me that he had spoken to his friend and we were to meet the doctor at his Washington office at eleven the following morning.

"Are you really sure about your friend, Dad? I mean, if this ever gets out, there's no telling who may get involved, and the last thing I would want is to become some asset for the military industrial complex."

"Mike, I know. I have to be cautious, but in my opinion I believe this is the best way to find out what in the world is going on inside that brain of yours. I'm taking every precaution I can think of, as your safety is my primary concern."

"Okay, Dad, let's see where things go after we talk to the doctor tomorrow."

17

After I had finished talking to Dad, I figured I'd better get back to studying. I couldn't quite put my finger on it, but there was just something a little unsettling about this meeting tomorrow with the psychiatrist. I had to believe that Dad had my best interest at heart, so who was I to second-guess him. Still, an ability like this to hear private telephone conversations was unnerving.

I really needed to concentrate on studying, but my mind kept drifting. Dad was downstairs with Mom, and I wondered if he had placed the binoculars back in his closet. I peeked out my door and listened. When I was sure he was still downstairs, I sneaked into his bedroom and grabbed the binoculars and brought them back to my room. I wanted to do a little more snooping and see what conversations I might be able to listen to.

I turned the lights off in my room and, sitting at my desk with the binoculars, I started searching around outside my window for anyone that might be on a phone. I spotted what looked like a teenager, standing on our corner. It was getting dark, but as he lit a cigarette, I could see he was talking into his cell phone.

As I brought him into focus, I could hear him talking to someone named Gary. He was giving him directions as to where he was, and suggested they could do the *transaction* there. I wondered what type of transaction he was talking about, but I had a pretty good idea.

It wasn't more than a couple of minutes later when a car pulled up to the corner and stopped. The kid stuck his head into the car window, and after a minute at most, the car left and the kid began walking away. He stopped for a moment and made another call, and this time the person on the other end asked if he got the *stuff.*

"Yeah, I got it, and it smells like some primo weed. I'm on my way to you now."

I had the feeling I had witnessed a drug purchase.

I then began to look up and down my street to see if I could see anyone else that might be on a phone, but no luck. Nothing going on, not even with the people across the street that I had listened to with my dad.

I figured as long as I was ahead of the game, I'd better return the binoculars to my dad's shelf, which I got done in the nick of time. Just as I got back in my room I heard both my parents coming upstairs. They were going to watch some television for a while before they went to sleep. I grabbed a book and opened it, as if I were studying, and just waited for them to pass by my room, knowing they would stop in to say goodnight.

18

After my parents called it a night I spent a few more hours studying, but then decided to call it a night myself. I knew I had the appointment with the psychiatrist at eleven the next day, and figured I might as well get as rested as possible so that all my cognitive functions would be working. I had no idea what type of tests he might put me through.

As I was taking a shower and getting dressed the next morning, I wondered what excuse Dad would give to Mom about where we were going. By the time I got down to the kitchen both of my parents were just finishing up with breakfast, and I caught the tail end of their conversation. I heard Dad telling Mom he needed some new golf clubs, and hoped he could convince me to go out with him to look around at a couple of golf stores in the area.

"Good morning, Guys," I said. "So are you ready to go to check out those new golf clubs, Dad? Yep, I would like to tag along for sure."

"Get your breakfast then, Son, and I'll be with you in just a few minutes. I'm just going to go up and get out of my slippers and get some shoes on," he said.

I grabbed a quick cup of coffee, and in no time Dad was ready to head out the front door. Mom never really knew where we were going, and I felt kind of guilty keeping her out of the loop, but I had to believe that Dad knew what he was doing. I finished my coffee and then met Dad out at the car.

As we drove into DC, I remembered, as a kid, how I would always be amazed at the national monuments, museums and sheer beauty of the place. As I grew older, I began hearing stories about clandestine operations and political backstabbing that went on daily, and in the back of my mind I always was wondering what it would be like to be a fly on the wall in a place like the Oval Office. I could only imagine the secrets that were contained in files that probably had been long forgotten, yet may have had an effect on the direction our country would be taking.

We were on our way to see a doctor that Dad had known for years. I recalled hearing Dr. Stevenson's name occasionally, and it was kind of strange having heard a name mentioned over the years, never thinking that someday I actually would have a need to be his patient.

Soon we turned into an underground parking garage. Dad had been unusually quiet on the trip over, so I figured he just had a lot on his mind. Little did I realize just how much he was concerned about the meeting that was about to take place.

As we pulled into a parking space, Dad turned to me and asked, "Are you ready, Mike?"

"Sure, Dad. Let's get this over with."

Dad locked the car and we made our way to the elevator. When the doors of the elevator opened on the eighteenth floor, we walked out onto gorgeous deep green carpeting that you just seemed to sink into. And I was impressed with the exquisite artwork hanging from walls that looked like polished mahogany. This place just reeked of money.

When we finally reached Dr. Stevenson's office, we found him leisurely reading a magazine in the waiting room.

"Good morning, Guys," the doctor said, getting up to shake hands. "Been a while, James. How's that golf swing coming along?"

Dad laughed and then introduced me.

"Ed, this is my son, Michael. And I already filled you in on why we're here."

"Yes, James. Delighted to meet you, Michael. Why don't you both come into my office and we can talk for a while."

We walked into an inner office where Dr. Stevenson took his place behind a massive high-end desk, while each of us sat down in one of two wing chairs that faced the desk.

"Mike—OK if I call you *Mike*?" the doctor began.

After I answered in the affirmative, he continued, "Your dad has given me some background on what has happened to you since your accident on the soccer field. Feel like filling me in?"

"Well, Dr. Stevenson, it was really strange. As my dad may have told you, I was in a coma for three days after being knocked unconscious. But what followed, I just can't explain. It seems after the accident, I've developed an ability to hear both sides of a telephone conversation as long as I'm looking at one of the individuals on the phone. I can hear both ends of the entire conversation as plain as day."

"Have you and your dad been able to prove this to yourselves without the shadow of a doubt?" the doctor asked.

"I think so, Dr. Stevenson. We took a ride yesterday into DC and stopped near several buildings, including the White

House. As long as I was within eyesight of the person talking on the phone, I could hear every word that was said."

"Mike, that's quite remarkable. After your dad spoke to me yesterday, I went through reams of medical literature and couldn't find one example of this ability ever being reported," the doctor said. "Before we go any further, can you demonstrate this ability for me?"

"Sure, Dr. Stevenson. What would you like me to do?" I asked.

"Michael, let's walk down the hall to an exam room."

Dad and I got up and followed Dr. Stevenson down the hall to a room with a one-way mirrored glass window that could be viewed from the hallway. He said the room was soundproof and was used for patient observations. Standing in the hallway, I would be able to see into the room, but would not be able to hear any sound made inside the room. He was going to go into the room and make a call to someone from his cell phone, and then after the call was over he would ask me what I had heard, if anything.

"You ready, Michael?" the doctor asked.

"Sure, Dr. Stevenson," I replied.

The doctor went into the room and turned his back toward me and the one-way window. I saw him take his cell phone out of his pocket, dial a number and then place the phone next to his ear. The call lasted maybe a minute, and after he finished, he walked out of the room and we all went back to his office.

"Okay. Michael, can you tell me who I was talking to?" the doctor asked.

"Dr. Stevenson, you weren't talking to anyone. You called the National Weather Service and were listening to the local forecast," I said.

At that point the doctor raised his eyebrows and his complexion had turned a steely gray. The look of shock on his face was something I had witnessed only a few times in my life, but that look of surprise was unmistakable.

19

I noticed Dr. Stevenson looking at my dad, and then he asked me if we could try this one more time.

"Sure, Dr. Stevenson," I replied.

We walked back to the treatment room, and this time the doctor asked my dad to walk down the hallway away from us. He said he would go back inside the room and make another call, this time to my dad. Again, the doctor walked into the sound-proof room and turned his back as he had before, and then proceeded to call my dad, or at least I thought so.

When the doctor had finished his call, we walked back to his office and while I had a seat, the doctor went out into the hall and called my dad back into the office. Dad walked in with a somewhat confused look on his face and took a seat.

"So Michael, what did I have to say to your dad?" the doctor asked.

I smiled coyly at the doctor and said, "You didn't call my dad. You called your wife and asked her what you were having for dinner this evening. She asked you if you were losing it, because she already had told you to pick up a special bottle of wine the two of you had tried at a restaurant last week."

At this point Dr. Stevenson had a look on his face that could be described only as astonishment.

"Michael, James, I've been a psychiatrist for thirty years, and never in my medical practice have I seen such an incredible gift. I can't even begin to explain to you what might have happened after your accident, Michael, but I am convinced, beyond the shadow of a doubt, that what I just experienced is nothing short of miraculous."

I looked at Dad and asked, "What now? Where do we go from here?"

Then I looked back at Dr. Stevenson and asked, "Is this a temporary or a permanent condition?"

"Michael," Dr. Stevenson said, "I never thought I would say this, but I am at a total loss. This is obviously a gift, and whether welcomed or unwelcomed, you have it, and only with the passage of time will we be able to determine its effect on you."

"So, Dr. Stevenson, are you saying just to live with it and see where things go?" I asked.

"Yes, Michael, that's my professional opinion. I can certainly do some added research and see if I can come up with some answers, but as things stand now, I would just accept the fact that you have this ability and see if there are any changes in the future."

"Ed," Dad asked, "is there anything that Mike should or shouldn't do at this point?"

"James, given Mike's ability, the only thing I would suggest is not going out of my way to use this gift in any way that might compromise others. Just keep it to yourself for now. I certainly wouldn't let anyone else know about this ability to listen in on private phone conversations."

"Thanks, Ed. We appreciate your time, as well as your advice. We'll just see where things go from here."

"James, stay in touch. I was happy to help if you want to call it that, but honestly, I have never in my professional life ever seen this unique ability before, and I seriously doubt I ever will again. Have a great day, Guys."

As we left the doctor's office, I asked Dad what we were going to do. Dad seemed really deep in thought and simply replied, "Let me think about it, Mike. At this point I have a million and one thoughts going through my head."

20

We finally arrived back home and I was somewhat concerned that Dad had been as quiet as he had been on the trip back. That was really out of the character for him, as he was usually pretty jovial. I figured I would talk to him a little later just to see what was on his mind. Mom was in the kitchen peeling potatoes that she would boil later to make her killer mashed potatoes for dinner. She liked to get that trivial task out of the way ahead of time, and would leave them soaking in water until she was ready to start on dinner—she never would use those dehydrated potatoes that came in a box. Only the real deal for Mom, and I definitely could taste the difference.

I headed back up to my room to get some more studying done before my first finals test that was coming up on Wednesday. After about an hour of study, I noticed Dad was outside watering Mom's favorite flowerbed, so I thought this might be as good a time as any to have a talk with him. As I walked downstairs, Mom was still in the kitchen, so I saw my chance to talk to Dad. I walked outside, and as Dad saw me walking over to him he asked how I was doing and how my studies were coming along.

"I doubt I'll have any problems with my finals, Dad, but I did want to talk to you about your friend, Dr. Stevenson, if that's okay?"

"Mike, I've given this a lot of thought, and at this point I think it best that you not use your ability at all, and just concentrate on school. I'm going to talk to Ed again tomorrow from work and see if he might have any further information for us."

"Sounds like a plan, Dad. But I can't shake this uneasy feeling I have about telling an outsider about this gift, even if he *is* a doctor and a friend."

"Mike," Dad said, "you may be right, and that's a concern for me as well. But we're just going to have to wait and see what happens over the next few days. I'm sure Ed will be able to come up with something for us."

"Well, Dad," I said, "if you really think that's the best way to go about things, I'll leave it in your hands."

"Mike, just remember, not a word to anyone else about this, okay?"

"Sure, Dad. Understood. I'm not about to tell anyone else."

With that, I went back to my room and returned to my studying. It would be several hours before dinner was ready so the time would be best spent studying, if nothing else, just to get my mind off the day's events.

*****

"NSA Switchboard, how may I direct your call?"

"This is Dr. Stevenson calling for Colonel Bridgewater."

"Thank you. Please hold."

"Good afternoon, Ed. Haven't heard from you for a while."

"Hi, Sam. Have you got a couple of minutes?"

"Sure, Ed. What's on your mind?"

"I just had one of the most remarkable experiences in my thirty years of practice. I know I'm betraying a confidence, but I believe this is really an amazing case."

"Maybe we should switch to a secure line. Hold on. . . . Okay Ed, go ahead."

"A long-time friend has a son that was in an accident resulting in head trauma, and ended up in a coma for three days. When he awoke, he had the ability to hear both ends of a telephone conversation as long as he had direct eye contact with one of the individuals that was talking. His dad even had him use a pair of binoculars, and he could do the same thing watching someone talking on a phone five miles away."

"Ed, its mid-Sunday, you drinking already?"

"Sam, this is the real deal. I had the father and his son in my office just now and tested him. Trust me. I wouldn't waste your time otherwise."

"Ed, if what you say is true—and I don't doubt you for a minute—but this kid, at best, could well become an asset, and at worst, a national security threat. Do you follow what I'm saying?"

"Yes, Sam, but I doubt the father will want to cooperate with any government agency."

"Let me worry about that, Ed. What's the kid's name?"

"Sam, I made a promise to my friend that this wouldn't go any further than what happened today in my office. I just can't get them involved in this. On second thought, it was probably a mistake even to tell you about this."

"Look, Ed, whatever your reason for calling me, the cat is out of the bag. If this kid has this ability, do you realize how our government could be compromised?"

"Yes, Sam, that's why I called you; but I'm not sure I should have broken the trust between doctor and patient."

"It never stopped you before, and you know we pay well, Ed. What type of financial incentive are you looking for?"

"Damn it, Sam. You just love dangling those golden parachutes, don't you? Look, give me a few days and let me talk to the father, and maybe I can convince him to come in on his own."

"Ed, you have twenty-four hours. Then we move."

"Understood, Sam. I'll be in touch."

*****

21

It was another restless night for me. I just had this strange feeling about Dr. Stevenson, but it was now Monday morning and I guess the best Dad and I could do was to wait for the doctor to get back to us. My doctors at the hospital told me I couldn't drive for another week, so I would have to catch a ride to get my finals taken care of. I left a message for my friend, Paul, and was waiting for him to get back to me. I didn't want to have to ask Mom to take another day off from work.

Dad had already left for work at the Pentagon and Mom was just heading out the door, so for now I was left to my own devices. I was tired of studying. At this point it probably would just be overkill. I know what my dad had said about not using this ability I had, but I couldn't resist just opening my curtains and looking out to see what was going on in the world. As I looked up and down our street, a black SUV was just turning the corner, and to my surprise, it parked right across the street from our house. I figured someone was going to pay a visit to the military people that lived across the street, but no one got out. The two men in the SUV were just sitting there, both staring at our house. What was going on here, I wondered.

At that point I couldn't resist hurrying to Dad's closet to grab his binoculars. When I returned to the window, the man in the passenger seat was just taking out his cell phone. As I focused on him, I could hear every word he was saying, and my skin began to crawl.

*****

"We have the house, Colonel Bridgewater. Is there anything you would like us to do?"

"No. I'm waiting to hear from the kid's doctor. I'll make my decision after I talk to him. Just head back to home base for now."

*****

As the SUV pulled out and left our street, my hands were shaking so badly I had to put down the binoculars, otherwise I would have dropped them and Dad would kill me for sure. I wasn't quite sure what I had to do, but there wasn't any doubt that I somehow was the focus of their attention.

I just couldn't contain myself any longer and decided to give Dad a call on his cell phone.

"Hi, Dad, can we talk for a minute?" I asked.

"Sure, Mike. Are you okay?"

"Dad, something really strange happened a few minutes ago. I was sitting in my room and had borrowed your binoculars."

"Mike, stop right there; I told you to let this go for now until I heard back from Dr. Stevenson, didn't I?"

"I know, Dad, but I saw this black SUV pull onto our street and then park right across the street from us. I was watching one of the men and he got on his cell phone. Dad, do you know anyone by the name of Colonel Bridgewater?" I asked.

Dad's phone went silent for what seemed an eternity.

"Mike, did you say Colonel Bridgewater?"

"Yes, Dad. That was the name. Do you know him or have you heard of him?"

"Mike, do nothing else and don't go anywhere. I'll talk to you when I get home, okay?"

"Sure, Dad. I'll stay right here."

After I hung up from talking to Dad, I wasn't sure which was racing faster, the thoughts in my head or my heart beating like a drum. As I thought about what had just happened, I had this sinking feeling that Dad's friend, Dr. Stevenson, was somehow involved in this, but I would have to wait for Dad to get home before I could get an answer.

The last thing I wanted to do was place my family in jeopardy, and the more I thought about it the more I was convinced that Dad's friend had probably broken his trust and must have contacted someone who would have an interest in my abilities. At this point I was feeling as if I would be to blame for anything that might befall the family.

As time passed, it was getting close to time for Mom and Dad to come home from work, and at some point Dad and I would have to discuss what happened today without Mom catching on. I had this very uneasy feeling in the pit of my stomach, that in some way my life and that of my family were going to change in a dramatic way. I just never had a clue just how dramatic the change would be.

At best, I had to keep a poker face for Mom, and at worst, I was just waiting to find out from my dad just who this Colonel Bridgewater was and what agency he might be connected to

After Mom and Dad arrived home and pleasantries were out of the way, Mom said she would get dinner going and Dad motioned to me to meet him in the back yard.

22

We had a couple of large oak trees in our back yard that provided a great deal of shade, so Dad and I sat on two lounge chairs under one of the trees. Both my parents loved to read, and sitting under the shade of the trees while they read was a welcome respite for both of them and helped them to unwind from their fairly stressful jobs.

"So Mike," Dad said, "tell me again what happened today when you saw the SUV stop across the street."

"It was just as I said, Dad. This black SUV parked across the street. I first thought they might be going to see the neighbors, but when it was clear they both were focusing on our home, I knew something strange was going on."

"Mike, while it was a concern in bringing your gift to the attention of Dr. Stevenson, I'm beginning to think that he may have said something to this Colonel Bridgewater you heard on the call."

At that moment, Dad's cell phone rang—and it was Dr. Stevenson.

"Hi, James. It's Ed. How is Michael doing?"

"Ed, he's doing okay, but the question I have for you is, for how long?"

"What do you mean, James?"

"Ed, did you talk to anyone after we had our meeting yesterday?"

I could hear Dr. Stevenson on the other end fumbling around for an answer.

"James, we've been friends for a long time, and I never would place you or Mike in harm's way. But in being totally honest with you, I did talk to a Colonel Bridgewater, and mentioned to him only that I had experienced a remarkable event that I wanted to research. But when I arrived at my office this morning, I knew I had made a mistake, because all of my files were thrown all over the office. The place looked like a bomb had gone off."

"Ed, had you created a file on Mike and his abilities?"

"I had only written down some notes, but the file did have the family's name and address on it. Is there something wrong, James?"

"Ed, of course there is something wrong! You promised me that this would be held in total confidence. What in the world were you thinking when you spoke to Bridgewater? There was a black SUV parked across the street from our home earlier. Mike was home and caught the conversation one of the people in the car was having with Bridgewater."

"James, I admit it was probably the wrong way to go about this, but as I said to you and Mike when you were in the office, given Mike's abilities, he could be viewed as a security risk. But believe me, James, I never gave Bridgewater any information on names or addresses."

"Well, Ed, I guess when the government feels strongly enough about something they just go to the source. Obviously someone broke into your office and found Mike's file with both a name and an address. Why in the world would you think a black SUV would turn up less than 24 hours later and scope out my home, you asshole?"

"James, I'm so sorry. I admit I had left Mike's file right on my desk. Is there anything I can do to make this right?"

"Ed, you've done enough already! Now my son, as well as my wife and I, probably have targets on our backs."

Dad's face was getting redder by the minute. I placed my hand on his arm and told him to stop yelling or Mom would hear him.

"Damn you, Ed!" Dad continued. "I really thought I could trust you, and now I have NSA spooks who know where Mike lives. Do you realize what kind of position this puts us in? I don't know what possessed you to call Bridgewater, but if that prick ever thinks he's going to use my son as a lab rat or worse, he's got another think coming."

"James, what are you going to do?"

"Let me worry about that, Ed. And as far as our friendship is concerned, it's over! And I don't want to hear from you again. I have a good mind to report you to the state medical ethics committee, but honestly, I have matters of greater importance to take care of. Go fuck yourself, Ed, and never call me again!"

With that, Dad pressed the end-button on the phone, with much more force than necessary. In all my life I never had seen Dad get this upset before. And of even greater importance was where we would go from here. Dad and I just looked at each other for a moment; then he said, "Mike, I need some time to think and figure out what we're going to do next."

"Next, Dad? I thought *next* was taking my finals this week," I commented, trying to lighten up the situation.

"Mike, just sit tight for now. I really have to think this through. The last thing I want to see happen is for you to be picked up off the street, or at school, or even here at the house—and never see you again."

"Are you serious, Dad? I mean, shit like this happens only in the movies. Well, doesn't it?" I asked.

Dad could only let out a long sigh. He told me to go get ready for dinner and cautioned me again, "Remember, not a word to Mom about this."

I headed to the house and could smell Mom's favorite Italian sauce bubbling away. As I entered the kitchen, she told me she had everything just about ready, and asked if I would set the table.

Dad finally walked in through the back door and Mom told him to get washed up for dinner, which was almost ready. When Dad joined us in the dining room, if I looked hard enough, I swear I could see steam coming out of his ears.

"Anything wrong, dear?" Mom asked.

"No, Lois, just a hard day at the office. I know there's going to be another fight on Capitol Hill about procurement for a Navy project. I have to make the rounds tomorrow and try to grease the skids to get senate approval, which is going to be like pulling teeth, but I think I can get my point across."

After dinner I told Mom I was going to do some studying, and as I got up from the table, Dad looked at me as if he wanted me to know we had to talk again.

23

It wasn't long after returning to my room that Dad came in to talk to me.

"Mike, I can't apologize to you enough for what happened with Dr. Stevenson. I misplaced my trust in Ed, but now we've reached a point of no return. If you stay here, there isn't any doubt in my mind that eventually Bridgewater's people are going to come after you. If they can't find you, then the heat is going to be placed on your mother and me to force you to come out of hiding."

"Dad, what are you saying?" I asked.

"Son, your life is never going to be the same. I'm not even sure the life you planned for yourself is even going to be possible at this point. This Bridgewater character is involved deeply in covert intelligence with the NSA, and I know he will stop at nothing to get what he wants, regardless of the people that may be unlucky enough to get in his way."

"Dad, are you serious?" I asked. "What am I supposed to do? I can't hide from these people for the rest of my life. Besides, we don't even know if this ability is temporary or permanent."

"Whatever it may be, Mike, Bridgewater wants to get his hands on you, and I'm not going to let that happen. Give me about a day, and I will have worked out some plan that will keep you safe."

Dad gave me a hug and assured me everything would be all right, and then left my room. I had a million-and-one thoughts going through my head. What about school, my career as a microbiologist? What about all of my friends, and the guys on the soccer team?

It seemed that this newfound gift was rapidly turning into a nightmare of historic proportions. I was not only in some type of danger myself, but I was concerned for my parents. The last thing I wanted to see happen was for them to be involved in this.

As I sat on my bed I tried to understand the gravity of what was happening, yet at the time I doubt if any of this really had begun to sink in. Would my own government go to such lengths to secure an asset? Was there no limit to how far they would go to obtain such an asset, regardless of who might get in their way?

I had no way of knowing how all of this eventually would turn out, but I had total faith in my dad, and knew he would come up with some plan. I was just heartbroken that if my worst thoughts came true, my life, and the one I had planned for myself, would never be the same. That was a life I wasn't looking forward to.

I tried my best to get back into studying for my finals, but at this point I was just too upset to think about anything other than how the different scenarios might play out. It was starting to get dark now, so I decided to close my curtains and turn on my desk lamp, but before I did, I looked outside. Sure enough, that same black SUV was parked across the street again, but this time, one of the men in the car got out and started walking over to our front door. I decided maybe it was best if I didn't turn on my lamp just yet.

I heard the bell ring and then saw Dad walk downstairs to talk to whoever was at the door. I couldn't hear what was being said, but as soon as the conversation was over, I saw the man leave our porch and head back to the SUV and then drive off. I waited a few minutes and heard Dad and Mom talking.

"Who was that, Jim?" Mom asked.

"Just a messenger that was sent to remind me of some important meeting I have to attend tomorrow, Lois. We'll have to talk about this later."

Mom then went back into the kitchen where I think she was creating another one of her great apple pies, as I could smell the cinnamon and apples cooking away. Dad came back to my room and closed the door.

"Mike, I had a visit from one of Bridgewater's agents, and they asked where they could find you to ask you a few questions. I told them that you were out with friends. He handed me a card with his phone number on it and said when you returned to give him a call."

"What should I do, Dad?" I asked.

"Do nothing for now, Mike. Just stay in the house. You don't have your first final for a couple of days, so just give me a little time, and I'll figure something out."

"Okay, Dad. I'll do whatever you need me to do."

Dad left my room, but I had a funny feeling that sooner or later he would have to take Mom into his confidence, as things were just getting too crazy at this point. My world was being turned upside down, and the only thing that was keeping me grounded was the belief that Dad would have some type of miracle plan that would keep all of us safe.

Mom and Dad soon retired to their bedroom, and I could only imagine the conversation they were having. Dad never had kept any secrets from Mom, but this was different. I knew Dad was really taken with this ability I had, and I also knew he would take all precautions to make sure this gift wouldn't be exposed to the wrong people. But in the end it was his own lifelong friend that had opened Pandora's Box, and Dad had just ended that friendship, which underscored how concerned he was about my wellbeing.

I had closed my curtains after the SUV left, but I never even bothered turning on a light in my room. I could only imagine what these people had in their bag of tricks that might give them some indication that I was home. I got undressed and ready to call it a night, but I just couldn't shake this feeling that my life and that of my family, as well as the lives of those I considered my friends, were all going to change in ways I had never imagined.

24

As morning arrived, I was awakened by the sound of the front doorbell. I looked over at my clock and it was only six-thirty in the morning. *Who in the world would be calling this early*, I wondered. Then I guess it was shear instinct, but I jumped out of bed and moved the curtain covering my window slightly, and sure enough, the black SUV was parked across the street again. My first thought was that these people would stop at nothing in order to get whatever it was they wanted.

I walked over to my door and cracked it enough to overhear what was being said. Dad sounded pretty calm, but I could hear a man's voice being raised, and he didn't sound all that happy. I knew that Mom had to be up, and at this point would probably give Dad the third degree as to what in the world was going on.

I waited for the man to get back into his car and leave before I decided to go downstairs. I slipped on a pair of sweat pants and a tee shirt and headed to the kitchen. Mom was already in tears, and I figured Dad had started filling her in on the events of the last few days.

"Morning, Guys. How's everyone today?" I asked.

I just played dumb, as I didn't know just how much of this crazy ride Dad had revealed to Mom.

"How could you both have kept this information from me?" Mom asked, in a highly exasperated tone of voice.

I looked at Dad, who seemed to be cool as a cucumber as he continued explaining to Mom what had been going on.

"Lois, I know in retrospect I should have said something to you, but we had to be sure that this gift Mike has was the real deal, and the only way I thought I could get to the bottom of this was meeting with Ed Stevenson. I just never believed in a million years he would have opened his big mouth to others, betraying our trust in him."

"James, what are we going to do? You know as well as I do that once these people latch onto something they never let go. What about Mike's life? And his school? And his career? Is he always going to be running from these people? Would it just be best to let them test him, or whatever they want to do?"

"No, Lois. We're not turning our son over to Bridgewater. I know full well that our son's life is going to change radically—and so will ours—which is why I have been giving this a great deal of thought. I told the agent this morning that Mike didn't come home last night, that he stayed with friends, but I didn't know which ones. All I want to do is buy us some time so that I can make arrangements for Mike to disappear."

"Dad, just where am I supposed to disappear to?" I asked.

"Mike, I'm working out the final details, and the three of us will talk about it a little later today. I'm just waiting for a call from a friend."

"What friend is that, Dad? The last one didn't do us any favors."

"I'll fill you both in as soon as I can tighten up some loose ends. I stopped at a store yesterday and picked up a few of the untraceable Tracfones. Now I'm waiting for a call from someone I know that can help us."

Dad got up from the kitchen table and went into the den. As Mom and I were sitting at the table, she placed her hand over mine and said, "I have every confidence in your father, Mike. He'll make the right decisions—I just know he will. And whatever the outcome, I know he has your safety upmost in his mind."

I guess after hearing Mom say that, I felt a little better; but this ability of mine was really turning into a shit show, and the last thing I wanted to do was cause my parents any further grief. The best I could do at this point was just to wait to see what Dad had planned, and take things from there. What I feared the most were these people coming back and storming the house looking for me, and I just didn't want to put my parents though that.

As I got up from the table to head back to my room, I gave Mom a kiss and told her not to worry, that everything was going to turn out all right. Truth be told, I was scared shitless, and had no idea what was going to come next.

25

After getting back to my room, I closed the door and just wanted to think. I wondered what my options could be. What could Dad have planned that would keep me from these maniacs, who would stop at nothing to get what they wanted—namely me? Was this ability I had something that would last a lifetime, or was it just some temporary aberration?

So many questions with very little in the way of answers. The best I could do at this point was to stay out of sight, but I wondered just how much longer this game of hide-and-seek could go on before the folks looking for me suspected something was going on, which could result in making their move sooner rather than later.

After a couple of hours of non-stop speculation on my part about different scenarios, Dad knocked on my door and asked me to meet with him and Mom in the living room. I headed downstairs right behind him, and then Mom joined us. As we all took a seat, Dad began to lay out his plan.

"Mike," Dad said, "do you remember Uncle Charlie?"

"Dad, I vaguely remember him. I think I was only seven when he passed away unexpectedly."

"Well, Mike, my brother and I had an old fishing friend that we used to catch up with out in Crosby, North Dakota.

He doesn't live there now, but he still has a cabin out there in the middle of nowhere. His name is Frank Queensbury, and I gave him a call on a secure line. I told him you wanted to do some fly fishing in that area and asked him if you could stay at his place for a couple of weeks. He just called and told me the place is yours."

"North Dakota, Dad?" I queried. "How in the world am I supposed to get to North Dakota, and how long am I going to have to stay in no-man's land?"

"Mike, I don't know how long you might have to stay, but I'm going to try to pull some strings with people I trust, and see if I can get these people off our backs. Frank said he always leaves the keys to the place with a neighbor, Martha McBride, who lives a few miles away, so you can pick the keys up from her. She's already getting the place ready for you. I'm going to mail a check to her for her time and trouble, and she'll have the place fully stocked for you."

"But Dad, how will I know what's happening? How will I be able to stay in touch with you and Mom?"

"Mike, I purchased several of these non-traceable phones, Dad said, as he handed me two Tracfones. Take these with you, and that should take care of communication. I bought some for your mom and me to use also—and I will give you the numbers. So if you have to call, don't use our house phone or our cell phones, but call us on one of our Tracfones."

"Okay, Dad. Got it. But how am I going to get there?"

"Well, it's going to be a little tricky to pull off, but I have that worked out, too. I don't want to use the airlines, because the NSA might already have put out an alert for you and may have you picked up the minute you check in with the airline.

So I need to get you on a train to Chicago. From there I have arranged for you to go the rest of the way by bus. But first I need to get you out of here under the cover of darkness. There is only one direct train out of here from Union Station to Chicago. It's an overnight train, and scheduled to leave tomorrow afternoon at 4:05 p.m.—and I have a ticket on it for you, with a reservation for a roomette. That will keep you mostly out of sight, and you should be able to get a little sleep. You will need money—I want you to pay cash for anything you buy—so I'm giving you ten thousand dollars in mixed bills: tens, twenties and fifties, along with one-hundred-dollar bills. But if you are apprehended before I can get you out of town, I don't want them to find this much money on you. So I purchased a small carry-on and put the extra money in it. I also stuck a couple of John Grisham's latest paperbacks in the bag, and wrapped everything in a couple of your old tee shirts. You're going to have plenty of time on your hands to read, and I know you enjoy Grisham's books. Unfortunately, there are no lockers at Union Station, so I locked the bag and checked it at the baggage storage area there—you'll find it near Gate A. I will give you the receipt to retrieve the bag, along with the key to unlock it. Also, here are five 20's to put in your wallet right now, because you will need money to get the bag out of storage, and also to buy a few meals.

"So how am I getting to Union Station?" I asked, wide-eyed.

"Well, I think it is safer for you to get out of this house tonight, while it is still dark. Sooner or later they are going to come here looking for you, and I'm afraid they will force their way in. These people will stop at nothing to get their hands on you. So I thought we would leave around three-thirty in the morning. And here's the tricky part. Just in case they are watching, I don't want them to see you in the car. The car is in the garage now, so I am going to pop the latch on the trunk, have you crawl into the trunk, and give you a ride to Union Station. I hate to do this to you, Son. I know it will be a little claustrophobic, but there won't be much traffic in the wee hours of the morning, so it shouldn't take too long to get there. And I just don't know how else to get you out of here without being seen. Once we get to the station, I will drive around the circle, and if there is no traffic at that point, I will make a quick stop on the far side of the circle, unlatch the trunk, and have you jump out and walk over to the station. If there *is* traffic, I will pull off on one of the side streets before you get out. Do you think you can handle that, Mike?"

"Dad, this sounds crazy, but I think you're right. It's the only way to get out of here, so I will try not think about it, and just do it!"

"Well, we should have a Plan B, in case for some reason this doesn't work out. So if necessary, do you think you could sneak out the back on your bike, and get to a Metro Stop, and make it to Union Station?"

"Sure, Dad. I can just go out P Street and hit the Dupont Circle Metro. The Red Line should get me there in about 10 minutes."

Okay, good. I hope that won't be necessary, but I am just trying to cover all bases. Here is an envelope to stuff in your backpack. Inside is a Metro ticket, your train ticket and your bus tickets from Chicago to Bismarck. Unfortunately you will have to change bus lines in Minneapolis, but the

Jefferson line is only about a 10-minute taxi ride from the Greyhound station that you will come into. And here is a card with our Tracfone numbers on it, and also Martha's number to use after you get to Bismarck. There is no bus service to Crosby, so she is going to pick you up in Bismarck. Then of course there is a key to your carry-on bag that is checked, and the receipt to get it out of storage. There's an hourly fee for storage, but you should have enough in your wallet to pay for that. But don't retrieve it until later in the morning, when there is more activity at the station. Then take it to the men's restroom, remove the money and put it in one of the zipped pockets on your backpack, and stuff the two books somewhere into your backpack. The bag is foldable, so if you like and have room, you can fold it up and take it with you in your backpack. If not, just throw the damned thing away.

"Oh, I almost forgot. You will need reading material before you retrieve the carry-on, so I bought you another book to stuff in your backpack now. "

Dad handed me the book, and I smiled when I looked at it, *The Brass Verdict*. Was he still trying to convince me to be a lawyer? He knew I liked Michael Connelly, and this paperback edition of the Connelly's book had just been released.

"James, I just have a terrible feeling about this," Mom chimed in, worried as usual about our plans. Wouldn't it make more sense to talk to these people and try to make some arrangement with them if they just promise Mike won't be harmed?"

"Lois, I wouldn't trust these people as far as I can throw them. This is the best way, and at least we will know that

Mike is out of their reach. I spoke to Monty Lafarge as well as Jack Hastings and took care of making some other arrangements."

Dad looked at me and continued with his advice. "Son, I know it will be a long day, but at least Union Station is a big place. So move around. Keep your baseball hat on, and when you go into a restaurant, sit with your back toward the door. Pull out your book, and if you don't feel like reading, at least keep your head down and pretend to be reading. When they call for boarding, you will have to stand in line to get out the gate to the platforms. Try not to be first or last, but somewhere in the middle of the line, and maybe keep *reading*, with your head in the book, the entire time you are waiting. Wherever you are, try to look around to see if there may be any surveillance cameras that you can avoid. I doubt you'll have to worry about it once you're out in the Dakotas, but follow my instructions to the letter."

"But Dad," I said, "these people probably will know what I look like. They have access to every database there is, and surely they can find a picture of my face from any one of a number of places. My school, driver's license—hell, they probably know more about me than I know about myself. Who are Monty Lafarge and Jack Hastings, anyway?"

"They're old friends your mom and I have known for years," Dad said. "They know the right people. Don't concern yourself with Monty and Jack right now. As far as people identifying you is concerned, the first thing you need to do tonight is to change your hair color from blond to brown. I picked up a box of hair dye, and Mom can help you with that.

"Is there anything else I should or shouldn't do, Dad?" I asked.

"Mike, just be sure to use only the phones I've given you. Do not use the mail or any other form of communication that might be monitored. If there's a need to get in touch with you, Mom and I will, but don't call the house phone or either of our cell phones. If something comes up, remember to use only our Tracfone numbers to contact us."

"James, do you really believe this is going to work?" Mom asked, in an exasperated tone of voice.

"Lois, it's the best we can do for now. I'm hoping that this will blow over and maybe I can get some people on the Hill to help me get Bridgewater off our backs."

26

Dad seemed to have covered all the bases, but I knew even the best of plans could always have a monkey wrench thrown into the works. As Dad was taking care of a few last-minute plans, Mom was helping me get my hair-color changed. I was always a blond, and seeing me as a brunette would be a trip. If any of the guys saw me like this, they would think I had lost my mind.

After the hair-color session was over, Mom gave me a kiss and a hug, and with tears in her eyes, said she was sorry that I had to have this burden placed upon me. I knew this was really affecting her, but I did everything I could to assure her that I would be all right. Somehow, I just knew that dropping out of sight was the only option I had, and the last thing I wanted to do was to place my parents in any type of danger. It was probably for the best that I leave, and I just hoped that in time Dad would be able to get some help in getting these people off our backs.

I needed to make this an early night if Dad wanted to pull this off in the wee hours of the morning, but I just had this sinking feeling that the people watching the house would be back at some point. I said goodnight to Mom and Dad, and tried my best to assure them that I would be okay.

After I got to my room, for some reason, I just started looking around at the little things that I had collected along the way while growing up. Old comic books, a coin collection I had started as a kid. There were pictures of me and friends from different places we had been to over the years. I even had my old Boy Scout Merit Badge sash, and remembered the days Dad and I would go camping and fishing together. All of this would have to be left behind, and yet in some strange way I felt almost disconnected from them, like they all were a part of some ancient history in my life. Nothing seemed to matter anymore. Not school, not my friends, not even the soccer team and the finals I was studying for. I just felt empty inside.

I packed a few clothes and toiletries in my backpack, and threw in the Tracfones Dad had given me. Lastly, I picked up the envelope with the important information I would need and placed it in a zippered pocket on the backpack. Then, as I got ready to turn in for what was going to be one of the strangest nights of my life, I kept asking myself, *why me*? Had I not tried being a show-off and diving for that ball at the soccer game, none of this would be happening.

I remembered my friend, Paul, once telling me that everything that happens to us happens for a reason. We may not know what that reason is in the grand scheme of things, but at some point in our lives, we come to an understanding. Maybe we finally do get to a point where we can reconcile the events in our lives and understand why things happened as they did. I'm sure for some people, they do find the answers they're looking for. Yet, for others, those answers may never come.

At this point it was already 10:30, and all I could do was let out a big sigh and try to get to sleep, as tomorrow would be the next day in my life—a life that was taking me in an unknown direction. As I drifted off to sleep, I was still asking myself, *why me*? It was then that I realized I was just happy to know there would be another tomorrow, and as long as I took Dad's advice, I was going to be okay.

27

I must have been sleeping for less than an hour when I suddenly was startled by a crashing sound. I jumped up out of bed and cracked open the door to my bedroom and I could hear Dad yelling at someone. I quickly ran to my window and saw that the black SUV was parked right in our driveway. Then I heard two gunshots in rapid succession, and Mom letting out a scream.

I knew Dad had a gun permit, but I couldn't tell who fired a gun, and I wasn't going to wait around to find out. My adrenalin level must have been going through the roof. I could think of nothing other than getting out of the house as fast as I could. I had no idea what had happened to my parents, but I just didn't have the time to think about it. All I knew was that I had to get out of the house myself and fast.

I grabbed my backpack and ran to the bathroom that I knew had a window I could climb out of and then onto a small porch where I could then jump to the ground. All I could hear at that point was Mom screaming and crying, and then I noticed a number of the neighbors' lights coming on. I had to move as quickly as I could without being seen. I grabbed my mountain bike that was sitting on the back patio and headed for the small gate in our back wall that not many people knew about. I was certain that I wasn't seen because as I looked back one last time, I saw the silhouette of a man standing in my room. They probably would have figured out I had been there and that they had just missed me, because it was obvious my bed had been slept in. I hurriedly proceeded through the gate, which opened to a narrow path with tall bushes on either side between two row houses, and came out on the next street. Then I jumped on my bike and pedaled as fast as I could, making a beeline for DuPont Circle Metro stop.

I arrived within minutes, and pulled my bike into one of the bike racks. Unfortunately I failed to bring my locks, so at least someone was going to end up walking away with a free mountain bike. I looked around one more time and didn't see anyone around this late at night. I must have caught the last train for the night. So far, so good. I grabbed my backpack and hit the escalator, still running down two steps at a time. *Please don't make me have to wait on the platform, Lord,* I thought. *Please send a train soon.* I saw a couple people on the other side of the tracks, and wondered if they were watching me. But no, they must have been a couple— they were interested only in each other. I was antsy, and walked back and forth until I finally heard the rumble inside the tunnel as a train approached. When the train stopped, I spotted a car with just one other person aboard, who seemed to be engrossed in a book. So I jumped on, and took a seat near the door. When the train stopped at Metro Center, several more people boarded, but no one who seemed to be interested in me. The doors closed, and we continued through two more stops, and then into Union Station. I had made the whole trip in 10 minutes flat.

I got off the train and slowed down and tried to relax, knowing I had reached my first destination and would have plenty of time to kill here. I found my way to the street level, and just sauntered around the entire floor, to get the lay of the land, so to speak, and then took a stroll up to the mezzanine level. One thing for sure, I wouldn't have to worry about a place to eat—I never had seen so many choices in one place. I went back down to the main floor and took a seat in a corner of one of the waiting areas outside the boarding gates. I thought I would sit there for a while and watch, to be sure no one was following me. *I must be getting really paranoid,* I thought. *Or maybe I have seen too many spy movies.*

I took out Michael Connelly's book and turned to the first chapter, but I found myself just staring at the book, not really reading it, as I began wondering what was happening to my mom and dad. A million-and-one thoughts raced through my mind, but one thing I knew: I had promised Dad I would follow his instructions implicitly, and I was in no position to do anything else at the moment, I finally decided to see if I could get absorbed in the book. It was one of the Lincoln Lawyer series, with Michael Haller, a defense attorney, who teamed up with my favorite character from Connelly's books, Detective Harry Bosch. And soon I was caught up in the plot.

28

I awoke with a start around 5 a.m. I was sitting in a corner of the waiting area, and somehow I had allowed my head to lean back against the wall and fall asleep. It took a moment to regain my senses and realize where I was. My book had fallen to the floor, so I grabbed it, then checked my backpack in the seat next to me to be sure I still had the envelope containing all my important stuff. Phew! Thank goodness everything was still intact. I looked around to see if I noticed anything suspicious, but everything seemed normal. Then I began wondering what was going on at home. Should I call them with my Tracfone? No, Dad said they would call me if they needed to get in contact. Oh God! Did I still have the Tracfones? I checked my backpack again, and found them still there, just as I had packed them.

There were several more people coming into the station now, so I decided to get up and meander around a bit. I could use a cup of coffee about now. I had seen a couple of Starbucks, but decided just to go over to MacDonald's, which was just across from the waiting area, and where I would have a little more privacy. I got my coffee and took it over to a corner seat, with my back to the entrance. I pulled out my Connelly book, put my head down and found my place, and began to get absorbed in the book again, while I sipped my coffee. Finally l decided I might as well grab some breakfast while I was there, so I went back and ordered another coffee and an Egg McMuffin, and brought them back to my little table.

Around 10 a.m., the station was crawling with people, so I figured it was a good time to mingle with them and pick up that carry-on Dad had stored for me. I tried to look nonchalant as I handed the agent my receipt. I was still a little nervous about interacting with people, but he hardly looked at me—just shoved the bag to me, and was ready for his next customer.

Now to be sure everything was there. I went inside the men's room, laid everything on a counter, took out my key and opened the carryon. Sure enough, just as Dad had said, there were the two Grisham books, and more importantly, a fat envelope, which I glanced into just long enough to be sure it actually contained the cash, then stored it in the zippered pocket of my backpack. I fumbled around and waited until everyone was out of sight, then dropped the bag into the trash, along with my two old tee shirts, which I should have thrown away a long time ago. I hoped whoever emptied the trash could make use of the bag—and maybe even the tee shirts.

So far everything had gone like clockwork. I had to hand it to Dad, he knew how to plan everything right down to the nth degree. I wasn't the type of person who always watched the clock, but as I left the restroom, I knew it was going to be a long day. Luckily there were many shops to wander around in, and a seemingly infinite number of restaurants. When lunchtime came, the place was packed with people, so I decided this was a good time to grab some lunch. I chose a place called *Charlie's Philly Steaks,* which happened to have a wall-mounted television. After I ordered, I took out my Tracfone to call home, but on second thought, I decided that would be a dumb idea. Still, all I could think about at the moment was what went on at home last night. Were my parents okay? Who was shooting at whom? I could only imagine what the neighbors on our street must be thinking.

As I sat eating my lunch, the news came on the television, and I was relieved when there was no mention of any disturbance that had taken place in Georgetown. So maybe my parents were okay. I might try calling them after I got on the train.

Somehow I kept myself entertained through the rest of the afternoon, and was pleased with myself that I had followed all of Dad's instructions, and had not raised any suspicion. Finally I heard the announcement that my train was boarding. I had chosen not to wait at my gate, but had been sitting in the waiting area of the next gate over. So I casually walked over to the gate for the *Capital Limited,* the overnighter to Chicago, and took my place in line. I was really nervous when I finally reached the head of the line and handed my ID to the agent, but he merely glanced at it, and then motioned me on through the gate.

I walked down a flight of stairs to get down to the platform, then strolled to the first agent I saw standing by an open door on the train. After I showed him my ticket, he directed me to my roomette, where I dropped my bag and practically threw myself on one of the two big chairs, which also would be converted to my bed for the night. This leg of my journey was going to take almost 18 hours, and the only thing I wanted to do now was to catch up on some much needed sleep.

Finally I heard a last call from the conductor, the doors closed, and exactly at 4:05 p.m. we headed out of the station and were on our way to Chicago. Even in a private compartment, I was a little paranoid about letting go of my backpack, so I stretched out on both the chairs, and curled up around my backpack, with one of the straps connected to my leg. No one was going to get their hands on it unless they took my right leg with them. It's funny the strange thoughts that go through our minds when we're stressed, and to say I was stressed at carrying around ten thousand dollars would have been an understatement.

All I really could do at this point was to wait to pull into Chicago, and then find the bus terminal and the bus that would set me off toward Crosby, North Dakota. I would just have to tough it out, nerves and all. At least I was now out of Washington, out of sight, and well on my way. I felt I could finally close my eyes and get some sleep.

I must have dozed off for a couple of hours, and when I awoke, the immediate urge to relieve myself came over me. I think I was ready to explode, considering all of the food I had eaten, plus three cans of soda. I picked up my backpack, eased open the door, and looked out to locate the restroom. I didn't see a soul, so I stepped out and made a beeline down the narrow hallway to the restroom. I couldn't believe just how much the human bladder could hold, but felt incredible relief afterwards.

There really was nothing interesting to see outside as the ride continued. We either were passing farmland or small towns. Middle America seemed as boring as ever, so I decided to try and get back to sleep. I could decide later if I wanted to leave my cabin to get some dinner in the dining car. Other than that, I would stay where I was until the train had reached Chicago.

I really tried to sleep, but I just had way too much on my mind. We probably had another twelve hours or so left before we pulled into Chicago, but it seemed I only dozed, on and off. As the conductor knocked on my door to see my ticket, I asked him if we would be arriving on time.

"We're still right on time, young man. We'll be arriving in Chicago by around eight in the morning."

I thanked him and picked up my book once again to try and do some reading. But all I could think about was not screwing up in some way, like being seen on a camera or even leaving fingerprints that could end up giving me away. I know it sounded like I was being overly cautious, but there was just too much at stake to screw things up now. I had read enough mystery novels and had seen enough television shows to have a pretty good idea how these government operatives worked, so I had hoped I could stay a few steps ahead of them and go completely off the grid.

Finally, as night began to turn to day, there was a knock on my door, and when I opened it, a porter—or whatever you called him—was there to serve me coffee, with a choice of croissants, Danish, or other pastries, which I really needed by then. I never did make it to the dining car for dinner the night before—I had been too paranoid to leave my cabin—so I was getting a little hungry.

As the train slowed down on the outskirts of Chicago, I made one more trip to the restroom. After I washed my hands, I brought back to my roomette a couple of wet paper towels and wiped down anything and everything I had touched just to make sure I left no prints. If these creeps were looking for me, the last thing I wanted to do was give them half a chance to pick up any clues as to my whereabouts.

Finally I could see we were pulling into Union Station in Chicago, and I could hear people moving about as the crew became busy preparing for passengers to deboard. At last I stepped off the train, and as I followed the exit signs to the taxi service in front of the terminal, I realized it was almost as massive as Union Station in DC, and my mind drifted back to learning in school all about the robber barons like the Rockefellers and Vanderbilt's that built a lot of the infrastructure for our modern day rail system.

29

Even though I knew the bus terminal was on Harrison Street, I had to rely on a taxi driver to get me there. Taxis were lined up right outside the door, so that was pretty easy. As I got in I told the driver I needed to get to the Greyhound Terminal on Harrison Street.

"Not a problem," he replied. "It's only about a mile away, so we should be there in no time."

He was right. I know it was way less than ten minutes by the time I had paid the driver, and was getting out in front of the Greyhound Station. Dad had told me I would have to get to Minneapolis first, and then change bus lines in Minneapolis to get to Bismarck. I walked into the station and began looking for buses heading to Minneapolis. My ticket said the bus would be leaving at 12:01 PM, but I checked with the agent to be sure there wasn't one leaving any sooner, and it was disappointing to hear him say, "Sorry, buddy. That's the only one out today. You are here a bit early, aren't you?"

"Well, I just came in on the train, so I have to take what's available." I almost had told him that I had just come in from DC—but decided I had better leave that part out. It was becoming second nature for me to give as little information about myself as possible.

"Then have a nice trip," he said, as I turned away from the window.

Nice trip my ass! I thought. *If he only knew!*

At this point I was beginning to feel a little more at ease and didn't feel as paranoid as I did back at Union Station in D.C. I walked around the station for a while, and noticed a lot of the shops and some of the bars that were open had televisions going. I would stop every so often to see if there was any mention of what had happened back home, but there was nothing. Around ten a.m., I had only a couple more hours to wait, so I finally bought another cup of coffee, and settled down in the waiting area with my book.

Time now seemed to be moving faster, and it was nearly time to board my bus. I found the gate I needed and headed out, and soon was seated comfortably on the bus, in a window seat, with my precious backpack stored on the rack above. To my relief the driver finally stepped onto the bus, sat in his seat and closed the door. That is when I realized there weren't that many passengers on the bus, and the seat next to me had remained empty, which gave me plenty of room to stretch out.

Of greatest concern to me wasn't where I was going, but what had happened back home. It was the two gunshots that really bothered me the most, and somehow I just had to know if Mom and Dad were all right. I also realized that I couldn't call the house, so I would have to give it some thought as to when I could use my Tracfone to make contact, and to find out what had happened after I left.

I already knew that this leg of my journey was going to take roughly eight hours, and we would be getting into Minneapolis around eight p.m. that night. I would have about a half-hour in Minneapolis to find my other bus and depart for Bismarck. Traveling was catching up with me again, as I began to feel my eyes starting to close. I got up from my seat and looked in the overhead compartment and found a pillow I could put to good use. But I just couldn't relax with my backpack in the overhead bin, so I pulled it down and did the same thing I had done on the train, wrapping one of my backpack's shoulder straps around my right leg. That bag wasn't going anywhere without me.

I must have slept for over six hours when I heard the bus driver's voice came over the P.A. system to announce we would be pulling into the terminal in Minneapolis in about thirty minutes. We had made some really great time. Most of the Midwest is pretty flat, but as we got closer to the city, it was amazing to see buildings reaching to the sky from such a flat and rural landscape.

We finally arrived at our destination, so I made a beeline out to the taxi service. I had only a half hour to get to the Jefferson Line station, so I hopped in a cab and asked the driver if he knew where the Jefferson Line station was, and asked him how long it would take to get there.

"Sure, I know it well," he said. "And I can have you there in 10 minutes. You look as if you are in a hurry."

"Well, I guess I am. I just came in from Chicago on the Greyhound, and had my fingers crossed that I could get to the Jefferson Line station in time to catch the bus to Bismarck, which leaves at 8:40."

"No problem at all. I'll get you there in plenty of time," he assured me.

By the time I had arrived at the station, the line already was forming to get on the bus. It seemed they were not sticking to the order specified on the ticket. It was first come, first served. So I began making my way to the end of the line, when I was stopped in my tracks by a police officer. At that moment all kinds of crazy thoughts were going through my mind, and I was nearly ready to hold out my hands to be cuffed, when he simply asked if he could show me something.

"Yes, of course, Officer. How can I help you?" I asked, as politely as I could manage.

"We're looking for a missing girl and wondered if you may have seen her."

At that moment I took a sigh of relief and replied, "Sorry, Officer, but no, I don't recognize her," as I looked at the picture he was showing me.

"Thanks for your time, sir. Should you happen to see her, you can contact the greater Minneapolis Police Department."

"Yes. I certainly will."

At that point I continued to the back of the line for the bus, which had just started boarding. When I finally took my seat, I looked out the window and watched as the officer went on his way. That was about as close as I ever wanted to get to authority figures. I was only too happy when the driver came back on the bus and said we were ready to depart.

As we began to pull out of the bus station, I noticed there were even fewer people that were traveling on this bus than the last. I would be surprised if there were more than 20 people on the bus. I also noticed that there were several military people, who, I assumed, were on their way to Minot, where there was a military base. So maybe that's why I had seen so many uniformed military people milling around the station.

I had placed my backpack in the overhead compartment this time, and now pushed my seat back slightly, as I just wanted to get a little more sleep. Still, the thought of what may have transpired back home was really beginning to eat away at me. I had to come up with some way of finding out what had happened. I knew I could use my Tracfone, but what if Bridgewater or his spooks were with my parents. It would be a dead giveaway.

As the bus continued its journey, I watched the lights of the city fade into the darkness, and soon had fallen asleep, with my mind still wondering how I was going to get in touch with my parents.

30

I must have dozed off for at least three hours, because it was almost midnight when I awoke. That meant another five hours before reaching Bismarck, so I decided to get out my book and do some more reading, but it was hard to concentrate. I kept thinking about how my life had changed so suddenly, and at this point in time, it didn't seem for the better. I had to believe that my parents knew what they were doing, and I took some solace in the fact that I had gotten this far. What could possibly go wrong now?

It seemed as if I had been traveling for days—and actually I had. I had left DC around four p.m. one day, arrived in Chicago the next, and now it would be another day before I arrived in Bismarck at five in the morning. I finally settled back down with my book, and began reading. I read and dozed, and dozed and read for hours, until finally the driver made an announcement that we would be arriving in Bismarck in about thirty minutes. I got up from my seat and removed my backpack from the overhead compartment and headed to the restroom to get cleaned up and ready for the last leg of the trip up to Crosby. I sure hoped Martha would be in Bismarck to meet me.

As I was going through some items in my backpack, I got out the envelope containing all the important information, found the card with Martha's number on it, and stuffed it in my wallet. That was something I couldn't afford to lose. When I finished up, I returned to my seat and had to wait only a few more minutes before the bus would pull into the station.

Once we arrived in Bismarck, it seemed the end of the line for all the passengers, as everyone scampered off in different directions. I went into the terminal, found the men's room, and splashed some cold water on my face, hoping that would help to keep my eyes open for a while. I glanced around, and didn't see anyone waiting around that might be Martha. I tried to remember. Did Dad tell me she would meet the bus? Or was I supposed to call her? How in the world were we supposed to connect? I finally decided the only thing I could do at this point was to call. So I sat down at one of the small tables, got out my Tracfone, and turned it on, hoping against hope that I would get a good signal.

Thank you, Lord, I thought, as a strong signal appeared on my phone. I really hated to call her at five in the morning. Still, I couldn't just sit there and deliberate about it all day, so I threw caution to the wind, and dialed her number, hoping I didn't wake her.

"Hello," someone answered, in a rather raspy voice.

"This is Michael, and I really hope I didn't wake you. Is this Martha McBride?"

"Michael! Yes, this is Martha, and you sure didn't wake me. We get up early out here. Where are you?"

"Well, I just arrived in Bismarck on the bus. Dad told me you would pick me up here, but I didn't know if you would be here or if I was supposed to call you at home.

"Well, Michael! I'm driving into the parking lot just outside the bus terminal as we speak, and I'm here right now to pick you up.

"Really? But I called you at home, didn't I?"

"Honey, you mean to tell me those people in Georgetown don't know how to transfer a call to their cell phones?"

"Oh, I gotcha," I laughed. "I guess I'm just not thinking so early in the morning."

"Well, that's understandable, young man," she said, and I could hear the smile in her voice. "So come on out the front exit, and I'll meet you with a Danish, and a thermos of hot coffee."

"Oh, that'll be great, Martha. I'll be outside in a flash. I'm wearing a black jacket with blue jeans, and I'll have my backpack with me."

I was beyond ecstatic as I grabbed my backpack and hurried outside to meet Martha. Once outside I spotted a little old lady stepping out of a rusted-out Ford pickup truck that had to be at least thirty years old.

"Howdy, Michael," she said. "That is you, isn't it?"

"Hi, Martha," I said, as she gave me a hug. "I'm glad I finally made it. It's a long way to Crosby—you must have had to get up in the wee hours of the morning to make it here."

"Well, to tell you the truth, I had some business to take care of in Bismarck, so I decided just to come in yesterday and spend the night at a hotel here. So it all worked out fine. Throw your backpack in the back, and climb in. Then you can take over this coffee and Danish that I scooped up from the hotel just before I checked out. I figured you might be a little hungry after being on a bus all night."

"You are right about that, Martha," I said, as I took the coffee and Danish from her.

She went around to the driver's side and got in, but when I tried to open the passenger door, it seemed to be stuck. Martha said to stand back as she pivoted in her seat and gave the door a kick. With the sound of metal on metal, the door flung opened and I climbed in, and we were on our way to the cabin.

"Martha," I asked, "just how old is this truck?"

"Michael, my last husband bought it brand new back in 19 and 75, and she's been purring like a kitten ever since."

I laughed and thought to myself, *This isn't exactly a purring kitten.* It sounded more like an angry lion, as there had to be holes in the exhaust system. You had to ride with the windows open because the fumes from the exhaust could choke a horse.

"Do you get out this way very often?" Martha asked.

"Not really, Martha. My dad said this was one of the best places to fish, so since I had time off from school I figured I would take him up on the idea of seeing something different, and Crosby sure seems to fit the bill."

What I did wonder was whether the cabin had electricity, or even running water. It had to be in the middle of nowhere. I just could not imagine my dad and his fishing buddies roughing it that much, but then again, they just might have.

Bismarck definitely had a western feel to it. Except for a few buildings that I'd say were taller than ten stories, the landscape was pretty flat. Life seemed to move at a slower pace. Men would tip their cowboy hats to ladies as they passed them by, and I could only imagine what life may have been like back in the day, when gun slingers and bank robbers were roaming the badlands.

I always enjoyed seeing other parts of the country and remembered, as a kid, going on camping trips with the family. It was always fun getting out of Georgetown during the summer months, and Mom and Dad would always pick a different place each summer to check out.

Even though it was early summer, I could still see small patches of snow dotting the landscape around Bismarck. Crosby was just a few miles from the Canadian border, and I was only too happy that my dad had the presence of mind to think of this location for me to hide out for a while.

Other than a ranch that I spotted here and there, I felt as though I was literally in the middle of nowhere. Rolling green hills as far as the eyes could see, and every so often I would see a dried out skull with horns from cattle that had been hung on barbed wire fences, like some badge of honor. Maybe that was the ranchers' way of showing off what they felt was the largest animal they ever raised, but it still kind of creeped me out seeing these sun bleached skulls hanging on fences.

31

On the way to my final destination to Crosby in Martha's old truck, we would be on the road for almost four hours before we reached the cabin. We made a couple of stops in what could be described as one-horse towns, with small, wooden buildings that were probably well over one-hundred-years old, wooden sidewalks, and even hitching posts for horses. What you didn't see in this part of the country were fast food chains, movie theaters, or mile after mile of strip malls. I couldn't even imagine any of these dots on the map having more than a couple of hundred people that lived in the area.

Finally we arrived in the tiny town of Crosby, the county seat of Divide County, which sits at the northeast tip of the state, bordering on Canada and Montana, with the Great Divide splitting it in half. Martha told me the fishing cabin was only three or four miles out of town.

The town itself consisted pretty much of only Main Street, with small stores, half of which were empty and for rent. This was definitely an agricultural community with an added emphasis on cattle ranching. Even stranger was the very apparent Canadian influence, as both the American and Canadian flags could be seen in several store windows. It reminded me of a trip I had taken with a few friends to see Niagara Falls in New York, where many of the shops on the New York side of the falls also displayed both flags. Many of the places in New York even accepted Canadian currency from the Canadian tourists.

"Well, Michael, Crosby is a pretty small town, with a population of no more than about 1500 people, many of Scandinavian descent. If you blink, you would probably miss it," Martha told me.

"Gosh," I said, "everybody must know everybody else."

"You probably are right. The people here are very friendly, and no one bothers you, which is just the way I like it. You won't find any fancy hotels like you see in DC, but we do have one golf course. Mostly you just see good Christian people making their living off the land, just as the good Lord intended.

"I hear you, Martha. What keeps you busy?" I asked.

"Well, Michael, I retired from the feed store in town years ago, and in the better weather I pretty much tend to my vegetable garden, and take care of a few laying hens I keep. This year I'm raising a couple of pigs as well. By the time late August and early September roll around, I will be keeping busy canning food to get through the winter months. I live mostly off my Social Security to make ends meet. At least my house has been paid off for years, and the taxes in these parts are pretty low."

"Martha, it sounds like you have everything you could possibly need."

And at that point I began to wonder again whether or not the cabin actually had electricity, or even running water, as it had to be in the middle of nowhere. I just couldn't imagine my dad and his fishing buddies roughing it that much, but then again they just might have.

"How much further is it now to the cabin? Are we there yet?" I asked, laughing.

"Not far, Michael. Maybe another half mile and we'll be there."

About that time Martha turned off the road we were on and shifted gears as the truck climbed up a dirt and gravel road that gave my kidneys a good workout. Just past a line of trees, I spotted the cabin, sitting near the edge of a lake. This had to be the place, as there was no other building around, and not another living soul to be seen.

She pulled up to the front of the cabin and said, "Here we are, Michael. Welcome to God's country."

Martha wasn't kidding. The cabin was small and was built with logs. A real log cabin, you might say. I noticed one stone chimney, two windows, and a front door.

"Martha, does the place have electricity and running water?" I asked.

"Why, of course it does, Michael. We may be in the boonies, but we're not living in the 1800's. C'mon and let me show you around."

32

As we both got out of Martha's truck, I thought to myself, *She's right. This really is God's country.* The lake was framed with beautiful trees on sloping hills and you just had the feeling of being at total peace. I walked around the truck and followed Martha to the front door of the cabin.

"Dang it, I always have trouble with this lock," Martha said.

"Here, Martha, let me give you a hand," I said.

After a bit of wiggling the key in the lock, the door finally opened. As we walked in I took notice of the dreary brown walls along with the dusty wide plank floors that creaked with every step we took. The place was really just one large room with an old-fashioned wood-burning stove to cook on. There were two bunk beds in one corner, a table in the center of the room, and a small sink off to one side. On the other side of the room was what appeared to be an enclosed wooden stall that had a toilet and a standup shower. I spotted a small refrigerator that seemed to be functioning, and when I looked inside, I saw that Martha had it full of food and beverages, so at least I wasn't going to starve to death. It certainly wasn't living high on the hog, but it would have to do until such time that I could find out what was going on back home.

Martha was a hoot. She was a small diminutive woman whose face looked like dried leather that was outlined by her silver hair. Her glasses had specs of mud on them and she seemed to fit right into the western motif, wearing a shirt fit for a lumberjack, and faded blue jeans that had seen better days.

"So, Michael, what do you think of the place?" Martha asked.

"Martha, it's everything I imagined and more. I'm going to have some fun fishing, that's for sure."

"Okay. Michael, I'm going to head back to my spread, as I still have to feed the chickens and the hogs, but if you need anything at all, just give me a call. I'm just a ways down the road and can be here in a minute."

"Thanks, Martha. I think I'll be just fine," I said.

With that, good old Martha headed back out to her truck, giving me a wave as she took off back to her place. Finally I was alone again with my thoughts, but first I just wanted to get settled in my new home-away-from-home.

I placed my backpack on the table and then walked over to the sink to see if the water was running. I turned on the cold water and honestly, I never had seen water that brown, so I figured I would let it run for a while just to get the rust out of the pipes, which luckily didn't take long. My next adventure would be making a fire in the stove so I could heat some water. There was a small stack of firewood next to the stove, along with some old newspapers I could use to get a fire going.

I found an old teakettle, along with a coffee pot, so I filled both with water and then proceeded to start a fire in the stove. I placed a small amount of wood into the stove and then lit a piece of paper to get the fire going. Little did I realize that the flue was closed—not until smoke began to fill the room. I looked around the flue pipe and finally found the damper. Once I opened it, the room began to clear. I just wanted to check one more thing, and went outside to make sure smoke was rising out of the chimney, and thank goodness, it was. The last thing I needed after coming all this way was to end up with carbon monoxide poisoning or burning the place down.

There was plenty of daylight left, as it was only eleven in the morning, but just in case, I decided to see if the one light bulb hanging from the ceiling actually worked. I pulled the little metal chain, and was relieved to see the light flash on, so at least I wouldn't be sitting in the dark tonight. Packing at the last moment for this unexpected trip out west, I had packed lightly, and basically had only the clothes on my back, along with a couple of pairs of socks and underwear. I figured I could give Martha a call a little later and ask her if she could give me a lift into town to do a little clothes shopping.

When I figured the stove was hot enough, I placed the kettle on the stove, and then took a look in a small cupboard above it where I found some plates, cups and silverware. I guess I had all the comforts of home, yet as the time passed, I just had to figure out a way of finding out what was happening back at my real home.

Martha had mentioned that there was fishing equipment out behind the cabin in a small shed, but I could take care of checking that out later. At the moment, all I wanted was a cup of coffee and time to think. Somehow I just had to know what was going on back in Georgetown. The last thing I wanted was for my parents to get in trouble over me, but it would be a total waste of time running a guilt trip on myself. After all, it was an accident I had in hitting the goal post that caused this series of events to take place, and I knew that as long as I had this strange ability that I would be a liability to anyone that knew me.

33

I was pretty much settled, and decided to take the cash my dad had left for me and hide it somewhere, as I didn't want to be carrying it around, and didn't want to leave it out in plain view in the cabin. Not that I expected to have any visitors, but even out here in the middle of nowhere, I wasn't willing to take that chance. I looked around and noticed that there were wide boards with spaces between them, so I stood on a chair and placed the bag on top of one of the boards. No one would ever know it was there except me.

I wouldn't be here long enough to get cabin fever, but I did want to take a walk around the place and maybe stroll around part of the lake. I hadn't made that large a fire in the stove, but if it burned itself out, I could always start it up again later.

When I walked out the front door, I was amazed to see several deer not ten feet from me that were grazing on clover that seemed pretty abundant in the area. No fancy lawns here. No streetlights. Just me and Mother Nature were all that could be found.

As I began walking along the lakeside I was still trying to think of a way to find out what was happening back home, and then it hit me. I could contact my best friend, Paul, and ask him to just take a ride past my home to see what was going on.

Again, my biggest fear was dragging anyone else into this mind-blowing mess, but I felt I had known Paul long enough to trust him. I knew I couldn't tell him why I had to leave town, but I thought I could give him just enough so he could fill me in on things, without placing him in any danger.

I decided to head back to the cabin and try giving Paul a call. As I started walking back toward the cabin, a hint of paranoia began to set in. If Paul didn't pick up, I wouldn't leave a message with a number for him to call me back. I just wanted to talk directly to Paul and not a machine.

After returning to the cabin I pulled out one of the track phones my dad had given me and tried calling Paul. I knew he already had taken all of his finals for the semester, though he may have been at soccer practice. His phone rang, but his answering machine picked up, so I opted not to leave a message.

Paul was probably at practice or chasing after some girl, but this was really starting to bug me. I had to know what happened after I had left the house. I also forgot that there is a one-hour time difference between North Dakota and Georgetown, so it was one hour later there, and Paul must have been at soccer practice. It was already one in the afternoon here, so I figured if I were going to catch Paul, my best chance would be later in the evening. At least I knew I could get cell phone service, even in the middle of God's country.

I really didn't want to bother Martha, but I had to buy some clothes to change into. The cabin didn't even have any towels either, so I guess I was going to put dad's money to good use. I pulled the chair back underneath the board where I had hidden the money, climbed up on it and pulled out two fifty dollar bills that would more than cover clothes, and even something to eat.

After retrieving the two fifties, I placed the bag back above the ceiling board and then decided to give Martha a call.

"Hi, Martha, it's Mike. I was wondering if I could ask a favor of you?"

"Sure, Mike. How can I help you?"

"Martha, I didn't really do much packing, so I was wondering if we could take a drive into Crosby so I could do some shopping. I'd also like to thank you for the use of the cabin, and I'd be happy if you would join me for dinner when we're in town—if you're up to it, that is."

"Mike, that's the best offer I've had in years. What time would you like me to pick you up?"

"Well, Martha, I don't know when the shops close in town. How would five o'clock work for you?"

"Mike, that sounds perfect, and I know a nice little place in town that serves the best food this side of the Mississippi, so let's make a night of it. I'll see you at five sharp. Okay?"

"Thanks Martha, I can't wait. And thanks again for the lift into town."

Well at least I got that out of the way, and rather than being caught short, I pulled an additional two twenty-dollar bills out of my bag, just to make sure. I knew my sleep schedule was off and I was still wound up as tight as a watch spring. I set the alarm on my cell phone to wake me in two hours, as I really wanted to take a nap. I had plenty of time before Martha would get here, and the couple of hours sleep would do me good.

The mattress on the bunk bed was pretty thin, so I took the mattress from the upper bunk and doubled it, which made sleeping a lot more comfortable. I think I probably passed out as soon as my head hit the pillow.

34

It seemed that no sooner had I closed my eyes that my cell phone alarm went off. It was four-thirty, and Martha would be arriving in about thirty minutes. I made sure the money I had for this journey was safely back behind the ceiling board, and just left my backpack on the bunk bed. I was a little apprehensive in leaving that kind of money lying around, but it was out of sight, and it didn't make any sense carrying it with me everywhere I went.

I had just finished splashing water on my face to freshen up a bit when I heard Martha's truck rumbling up to the cabin. Martha was a spunky eighty-something that had probably lived an interesting life. People out west seemed to be a different breed. They prided themselves on their independence along with a can-do spirit that you just didn't see back east. Here, life wasn't rushed, but rather embraced, and taken at a far slower pace.

As Martha pulled up to the cabin, I asked her if she had the key so I could lock the front door.

"Hi, Michael. Sure do. Sorry that I forgot to give it to you, and I also brought a can of WD40 to spray into the lock; hopefully that will help loosen the mechanism. Give it a little squirt and it should be a whole lot better by the time we get back."

I took the lubricant from Martha and sprayed it into the lock; then I inserted the key a few times, and sure enough, the lock worked perfectly. After I finished fiddling with the door, I locked up the cabin and we took off for Crosby. Martha asked me if I had ever been out west before, and I told her that yes, I had been, on several occasions.

On the ride into town, Martha began telling me about the good old days when thousands of heads of cattle would be brought up to this area where they would graze in the spring and summer to fatten them up, and then when summer turned to autumn, were herded south again to the ranches they came from. She also loved to talk about cowboys, along with some of the more famous names of bank robbers that used to roam the west. There was no question the old girl loved the area, and it certainly was steeped in history that seemed so far removed from life back east.

We finally rolled into town and Martha asked if I wanted to hit the men's store first, as they would be closing at six. She said she would meet me back at the store in a little while, and then we could go and get something to eat.

I walked into a place called *The Variety Market Place,* and while you wouldn't find designer jeans in Crosby, I was able to pick up a few pairs of Levi's and half a dozen tee shirts, along with a couple of dress shirts and socks.

After paying for my purchase, I walked outside, and there sat Martha, waiting for me. She said just to leave the bags I had in the truck, and assured me that no one would touch them.

"Really, Martha?" I asked.

"People in these parts, Michael, are not only honest, but if anyone were ever caught stealing they would either be shot or hung, their choice. "

"You know I'm kidding, don't you, Michael?" she said, as she let out a big smile and started laughing.

"Very funny," I replied.

"So, Martha, where can we get something to eat? I'm starving."

"Michael, we're going to head over to *Mr. K's Steakhouse*, right across the street. They have the best steaks you ever have sunk your teeth into."

"Sounds great, Martha. Lead the way."

As we walked in I couldn't help but notice the largest horns from a steer I had ever seen that were mounted above a long bar that we walked past before reaching the dining area. I was starving and couldn't wait to order. The waitress' name was Amy, and the first words out of her mouth were, "Howdy, Martha. Who's the hot young stud you brought along?"

I must have turned red as a beet. Martha introduced me, and Amy asked if I was from around these parts.

"No, Amy, I'm actually visiting for a while and thought I would do some fishing in the area."

"Well, we have plenty of lakes to choose from. After a few days of fishing, you'll probably have caught so many you'll be sick of seeing fish. Now what can I get for you two?"

"Amy, I think I'll have the eight-ounce tenderloin with a baked potato and a small house salad. How about you Martha?" I asked.

"Amy, just make that two, Honey," Martha said.

"Okay guys, coming right up. Would you like something to drink?"

"Amy, I think I'll have a coke. How about you, Martha"?

"Amy, make mine a coffee," Martha said.

It didn't take long for the food to arrive and I thought I had died and gone to heaven when I tasted the tenderloin— it simply melted in your mouth. Martha kept going on about the good old days in the Wild West, and as far as company is concerned, you couldn't ask for a better dinner companion than Martha.

35

We seemed to finish our meal in record time, and from the looks of it, I guess we both were pretty hungry.

"Martha, can I interest you in dessert?"

"Michael, they have some of the best chocolate cheesecake you ever have had. Want to try it?"

"Sure," I said. "Why not?"

Martha wasn't kidding. This cheesecake was as good, if not better, than anything I ever had back home. I asked Amy for the bill and was glad I had taken the two extra twenties. After the clothes shopping I had done, I had just enough left over to leave a pretty good tip. We finished up and then headed to the truck for the ride back to the cabin.

I guess I was pretty quiet on the way back, as Martha asked if the cat had caught my tongue.

"I'm just thinking about what's going on back home. I guess my parents are having a great time without me hanging around."

"Oh, you don't mean that," Martha said.

"No, I don't, Martha. Just kidding," I replied.

When we arrived back at the cabin, Martha said to give the lock on the front door a try. As I turned the key, the door opened effortlessly. Martha told me not to forget my shopping bags, which I almost did. Once I got them out of the back of the truck, Martha took off. As she was rolling on her way, she stuck her head out the window and said, "Just call, Mike, if you need something; otherwise I'll check in on you tomorrow."

As Martha's truck disappeared, along with the rumbling sound her exhaust made, I suddenly noticed just how deathly quiet it had gotten. It was just me and the great outdoors.

I brought the bags into the cabin, and it wasn't that I thought anyone had been there, but I checked, just in case, to make sure the money was still where I had left it. Yep, it was there, so now it was a good time to try again to reach my friend, Paul, back home.

I sat down on my bunk bed, grabbed my cell phone and dialed Paul's number. It rang three times, and just before his answering machine kicked in, Paul picked up.

"Hello."

"Hi, Paul, it's Mike."

"Dude, where in the world are you? I mean what the hell went on at your place. Are you okay?"

"Paul, it's a long story and I can't get you involved in this."

"What the hell are you talking about, Mike? Do you have any idea what went down at your home?"

"Paul, that's why I'm calling. Listen, I'm not going to stay on long. Can you give me any idea how my parents are?"

Paul paused for what seemed an eternity, and then asked me if I was sitting down.

"Yes. Paul, I'm sitting, but I don't think I'm going to like hearing what you have to say."

I could hear Paul's voice begin to quiver.

"Mike, we've been best friends for most of our lives, and I never thought…."

"Jesus, Paul—just spit it out already, will you?"

"Mike, I don't know how to tell you this, but your dad is dead."

As I heard Paul utter those words, my head slumped to my chest and my heart almost stopped. Unbelievable! What a shock! To say I was devastated would have been putting it mildly. Surely I heard him wrong.

"Mike, hello Mike, are you still there? Man, I am so sorry to have to have been the one person to tell you this. Mike, you have to fill me in, Man. It was all over the local news."

"Paul, listen to me. Just stop talking and listen. I can't stay on the line longer than three minutes. How is my mom?"

"Mike, no one knows where she is. My mom tried calling the house and the phone just rings. She and I took a ride over to your house to see if we could find out something, but there was police tape all over the place, and what used to be your front door was now covered with a piece of plywood. What the hell are you involved with, Mike?"

"Paul, I can't say any more than I already have. I'll try to get in touch with you later. I just have to take all this in. But not a word to anyone, not even to your mother, that I made contact with you. Promise me that, Paul!"

"I promise, Mike."

I hung up on Paul and just sat on my bed totally numb at the news Paul had given me. I tried piecing together the events of that night, and I distinctly remembered hearing two gunshots. Until I could get any further information from Paul, I just wanted to be alone with my thoughts.

A million memories started flooding back from better days. Mom and Dad trying to teach me how to ride a bike, Mom taking me as a kid for the first time to see Santa Claus at Macy's in New York on a weekend trip. Catching my first fish with Dad when I got so excited I fell out of the boat, and he had to pull me out of the water.

I kept asking myself why this was happening to me. Why, after a bump on the head, did I end up being cursed with this ability? Something inside me was saying my life would never be the same again. How could it after the series of events over the last forty-eight hours?

I could just hear my dad now saying, "Mike, stop feeling sorry for yourself." But if it weren't for this freak accident, I would still be home studying for my finals, with only a year to go before I started working on my master's in microbiology. As far as I was concerned, my life was over. My dad was dead, I had no idea where Mom was, and I was on the run from government agents that probably had less than stellar reasons for wanting to get their hands on me.

36

I needed to think, but the longer I thought about my position, the fewer options I seemed to have. It was still about an hour before sunset, so I decided to lock the cabin and go for a walk by the water. Maybe that would help me clear my head.

I found a large rock on the edge of the lake and decided just to sit down and try to figure out what I should do next. There was no one in my life that I could even think of dragging into this. Suddenly, tears began flowing down my face as the gravity of the situation finally seemed to hit me. I can't remember ever feeling so much alone and scared. I had no idea what my next move was going to be.

Trying to remember what had happened after hearing those two shots was a total blur. I knew my dad had a revolver. Maybe the crashing sound I had heard was the front door being bashed in, and then I wondered if my dad could have gotten a shot off before being hit by the second gunshot I heard. I just didn't have any answers at the moment, and in my current state of mind nothing made sense.

As the sun went down behind a stand of trees, I could still see my reflection in the water, but the image I saw did not portray my feelings, and the mess I had made out of my life. I just didn't have a clue as to what I should do next.

I finally got up from the rock I was sitting on and headed back toward the cabin. As I turned to take one last look at the lake, I thought I detected something moving on the other side of the water near the trees. This wasn't the moment I needed my mind playing tricks on me, so I told myself it probably was just a deer or some other animal, but just in case, I picked up the pace of my walking.

When I arrived back at the cabin, I fumbled with the key and finally got the door to open. After I walked in, I looked out the window, and with what little light was left, I couldn't see anything moving outside. I just couldn't start letting my imagination get the better of me, and I slowly began to regain my composure.

I took my jacket off and placed it on the one chair in the place and figured I would start a fire in the stove and make a cup of coffee. My mind was still reeling from the news Paul had given me, but I had to have some kind of plan and figure out what my next move was going to be. There were still some hot coals in the stove, so all I had to do was place a little more wood on the coals and soon it would be hot enough to get a kettle of water boiling.

The thought had crossed my mind to give Paul another call, but I wasn't sure it would be safe, even with the phones dad had given me. I just didn't want to take any chances, as I could only imagine the technologies that an agency like the NSA had at its disposal.

I had just placed the kettle on the stove when I thought I heard a branch crack outside. I didn't dare turn the light on, so I slowly walked to one of the windows to peak outside. I didn't see a thing moving, so I felt I still must be letting my imagination run away with me, and turned and headed back to the stove.

These old timers really had things figured out. I was amazed at how fast the water came to a boil on this antique. As I reached for my cup, I definitely heard something or someone approaching the front door. My heart started racing like never before. I looked around the room and the only thing I could find as a weapon was an old shovel.

Then it happened. Someone was knocking on the front door. Crazy thoughts started going through my head. How could the bad guys have found me—if in fact it was even them? Then I heard the knock again, but this time a voice called out, using my name.

"Mike Brewer! Mike, I'm a friend of your dad's. Can I come in?"

"How can I be sure you know my dad?" I asked from behind the door.

"Mike, I'm an old friend of your father's. We were in the Marines together. He wanted me to help you in case something happened to him. Please, will you let me in?"

I didn't know what to think, but he did know my name, as well as the fact that Dad had been a Marine. I cautiously cracked the door open, fully expecting it then to be blasted open against me, but all I heard was the voice again:

"Mike, I promise you I'm not here to do you any harm. My name is Jack Hastings, and we really need to talk."

I held the shovel in one hand and carefully opened the door with the other. This guy had to be well over six-feet-four, and was built like a brick shit house.

"How do you know me, and how in the world did you find me?" I asked.

"Mike, you can put the shovel down. I'm not here to hurt you, but to help you. Several days ago your dad got in contact with me. Would you mind if I sit down?"

"Sure, have a seat," I said. "You said your name was *Jack Hastings*. My dad never mentioned anyone by that name before.

"He probably never would have mentioned my name, Mike."

"Oh, now I remember. Just before I left home Dad said he was going to get in touch with you. Sorry. Guess I'm just so rattled at the moment that the name didn't ring a bell. Would you like a cup of coffee?"

"Yes, thanks, I'd love a cup of coffee. I've been walking around these woods looking for you for hours. Then when I was on the other side of the lake, I heard a truck pulling up and just waited around to see who it was."

"I still don't get it, Jack. How the hell did you know to come here looking for me in the first place?"

"Your dad loved you very much, Mike, and took some extra precautions in the event something happened to him after sending you off into hiding."

"Extra precautions?" I asked. "Like what?"

"Mike, you have a backpack, don't you?"

"Yes, I do."

"Can I have a look at it for a minute?"

"Sure," I said, as I handed my bag over to Jack.

I watched as Jack opened the top flap, and there, hidden in the seam of the cover to my backpack was a small wire that was attached to something else that looked like a transistor, or some sort of electronic device.

He pulled it out to show me as he said, "Mike, this is a GPS tracker that a number of agencies use in covert operations. Your dad was a whiz with electronics, and he was able to change the frequency on the device so only I could pick up the signal. I've been tracking you ever since you left Georgetown."

"This is unbelievable, Jack. You only see this kind of stuff in the movies."

"It's crazy stuff, Mike. You can't even begin to imagine what the government has at its disposal."

"Jack, I called a friend back home that I know I can trust. I had to know what had happened back at the house after I went on the run. Can you fill me in at all?"

"Son, this is going to take a few hours, and after I tell you the entire story, I hope your head doesn't just explode."

"I'm all ears, Jack. How about you start at the beginning."

37

"I know much of what I'm going to tell you, Mike, may come as a shock, but as your dad's best friend, I want you to know the truth. I can also fill you in on Colonel Bridgewater and his band of misfits, if you like."

"I'm listening, Jack. Let me have it all."

"Like I said, your dad and I were in the Marines together. After basic training, several of us were called upon to do some advanced front line work in the Middle East. Basically, we were trained and turned into spies for the military. Your dad and I were on a number of missions that gave us access to some of the best technology at the time. We did some things that I'm not proud of, but in the end, our government leaders and the top brass in the military felt these missions were necessary. They actually plan years in advance for any military action that is taken abroad."

"This sounds like some real cloak-and-dagger stuff, Jack," I commented. "Were you and Dad ever in any real danger, or were you just on fact-finding missions?"

"It's a lot deeper than that, Mike. I can't knowingly tell you what we did, but we believed it was always with the intent of keeping the country safe. When our tour was over, your dad left the Marines and went to law school. After graduating, he was asked by a high-up operative to work at the Pentagon as a liaison between the military and several key senators."

"Jack, I knew my dad worked at the Pentagon, but so did my mother. Was she somehow involved in these dealings as well?" I asked.

"Yes, she was, Mike. She was what was known as an *insider*. At a secret meeting, both your dad and your mom were asked to report to a private, non-governmental military group, which worked alongside of those in our government who wanted to see America return to the true rule of law under our Constitution."

"Jack, this sounds almost like some right-wing group trying to overthrow our own government. Is that correct?"

"No, Mike, It's not. You probably don't realize it—few people do—but without going too deeply into this, I will just say that our country is run by a shadow government comprised of some of the richest corporate and banking people in the world, and they're not all US citizens."

"Jack, yes, I've heard all the conspiracy theories, but never in a million years did I ever give any credence to them."

"Mike, our government has worked it down to a science when it comes to throwing cold water on those theories when they pop up on the internet. Having been generated by fringe groups, they're pretty much scoffed at."

"Jack, I don't really need to know any of the secrets, but I'd just like to know why this Colonel Bridgewater wants me as badly as he does."

"Bridgewater is a tool. He does the dirty work for others. Given the ability you have, you would be a prime asset that could well be used against our country. Mike, can you explain to me exactly what happened to you after your accident playing soccer?"

"Jack, all I know is that after I got out of the coma I'd been in for three days, I noticed I had this ability to hear both sides of a telephone conversation as long as the individual talking was in my line of sight. That's it."

"Mike, that is truly an amazing ability; would you mind if we did a little test so I can see this in action for myself?"

"I don't mind at all, Jack. What did you have in mind?"

"Tell you what, Mike. I'm going to go outside and make a call to someone. I'll have my back turned to you, but will remain in your line of sight. When I'm done, just tell me who I was talking to, okay?"

"Sure, Jack."

Jack walked out of the cabin and shut the door behind him. He must have walked at least one hundred feet from the cabin and then stopped, took out a cell phone, and made his call. I heard the phone ringing on the other end and then I heard a woman's voice pick up.

"Is he all right, Jack?" the woman asked.

"Yes, Lois, he's fine, and I'll go ahead with all the arrangements. Take care."

I couldn't believe what I had just heard. I was in total shock when I heard my mother on the other end of the call. Jack returned to the cabin and took his seat at the table.

"So, Mike, who was I talking to?"

"Jack, it was my mom. You said I was fine and that you would take care of making some arrangements," I said.

The look on Jack's face was one of total amazement.

"Yes, Mike, that was your mother, and she's okay and in a very safe place."

"Thank God for that, Jack. Were you and the people you're connected with responsible for keeping my mother safe?"

"Yes, Mike. After the incident that took place at your home, your mother was taken away by agents associated with Bridgewater, but we had people stationed in strategic places and were able to get to her before the SUV she was riding in could make it back to the NSA headquarters."

"And you are sure she is in a safe place now?"

"Yes, Mike. And it's my responsibility to keep you safe as well, and to get you out of the country."

"Jack, I think I've read one too many Tom Clancy novels. I can't believe that this stuff actually goes on without the general public even having a clue."

"Mike, your brain would really freak out if you knew the half of it, especially what goes on out at Area 51."

"Say no more, Jack. I'm having a hard enough time trying to process what you've already told me. I guess my last question for you is where do we go from here?"

"Mike, I'm going to have to disappear for about a day. Can I see one of the phones your dad gave you?"

"Sure Jack, here you go."

"Mike, I'll bring this back to you when I return, but do not make any other calls to anyone else back home. Do you understand me, Mike?"

"Yes, Jack, but what about Mrs. McBride? I know she's going to try and call me tomorrow; either that or take a drive up here to the cabin."

"I'm not concerned about her, Mike. That's okay."

38

Jack took the cell phone and left just as quickly as he had appeared. I had so much information going through my brain that my headache started coming back. I took a couple of Advil and hoped it just might be stress-related rather than some medical condition associated with my accident.

While I had a hard time believing a lot of what Jack had to say about my parents, things did start to make sense. As a kid growing up, I remembered several people that used to come to our home, and when they arrived, I was always asked to go to my room. I once stood on the staircase trying to listen in on their conversations, but Dad always closed the French doors to the living room at those times, and I couldn't hear a thing.

I always thought we were just as normal as any other American family, but that obviously wasn't the case. I wasn't sure what my parents were involved with, but at least now I knew Mom was safe and apparently in good hands. I really hoped I would get the chance to see her soon.

The stove was still going and it really heated the cabin up, so I figured this would be as good a time as any to take a shower and finally get some sleep. I walked over to the front door and locked the latch and then closed the really faded green curtains on the two windows.

It felt good getting cleaned up after all the traveling I had done, and all I wanted to do at that point was to get a really good night's sleep, so after my shower I dried off and slipped into a pair of sweat pants and my Georgetown sweat shirt. It was time to call it a night and just wait for Jack to get back to me.

After I crawled into my bed I just lay there and reviewed the events of the last couple of days. I wasn't really sure what to believe. I knew that Jack was a good friend of my dad's, and he obviously knew my mother. What I wasn't sure about was where he had gotten his information. It had to be either Mom or Dad, but honestly, it really didn't matter.

As I've thought so many times in the past, I believe there has to be some grand plan, some universal design that drives our lives in certain directions. I fully realized that we humans also have something called free will, that will allow us to screw up our lives as we choose to. Sometimes things work out, and at other times they don't.

What I had tried in vain to understand was why I had been chosen to have these mind-bending events take place in my life. I was beyond saddened that this gift I had was responsible for the death of my father, and that is a mental and emotional burden I probably would carry for the rest of my life. As I thought of my dad, I felt tears well up in my eyes once again.

"Dad, I know you're with me and always will be," I said softly, through my tears. "I hope you know how sorry I am for having caused this much trouble, and I hope you and Mom can forgive me."

It was getting late, but at least my headache had disappeared and all I wanted to do was close my eyes and get some sleep. I already had turned off the one light in the cabin, and as I began to drift off, I heard what sounded like a wolf baying in the distance. I guess this was what life was really like in the Wild West.

39

The sun was blasting through the windows in the cabin, so it had to be morning, but I didn't realize how early it was until I heard Martha's old Ford pickup rumbling closer to my location. I looked at a small travel clock I had brought with me and it was only six-thirty in the morning. I guess people here really got their day going early.

I jumped out of bed and unlatched the door. Martha was just getting out of her truck and was carrying something I couldn't quite make out.

"Good Morning, Michael. How ya doin' today?" Martha asked.

"I'm doing pretty good, Martha. What in the world are you carrying?" I asked.

"Darlin', for someone who came out all this way to go fishing, you sure travel light. My last husband loved to fish, but after he passed several years ago I kept his favorite tackle box. The fishing poles are in the back shed and I think these fishing lures will help you catch some beauties, unless you'd rather go digging for worms."

"Martha, thank you so much. That was really sweet of you, and they sure will be put to good use. Would you like to come in and have a cup of coffee? It won't take long to make."

"Sorry, Michael, no can do right now. I have a friend that's been ailing and I promised her I would drive her over to her doctor for an appointment this morning, and I'm running late now. I'll stop by later today and let's see how good a fisherman you are."

Martha got back into her truck and headed for points unknown, so I thought I might as well get the fire going in the stove and have some breakfast. Martha had filled the fridge, and some scrambled eggs sounded pretty good about now.

After the fire got going, I filled the kettle and found a frying pan in the back of the cupboard. Once the stove heated up I got the coffee and scrambled eggs going. Then when I got breakfast out of the way, I cleaned up the kitchen area, and got dressed, ready to start my day.

Since Martha had gone out of her way to bring over her husband's tackle box, I didn't want to disappoint her by not having caught anything. Besides, I had no idea where Jack had gone, and wasn't really sure when he would be coming back, so I figured I might as well try my luck at fishing. It was really a beautiful day as I headed out back to get one of the fishing poles. All I really was trying to do was to kill some time, waiting for Jack to return. I walked to the shed and when I opened it, I saw a couple of fishing poles and what appeared to be a large tarp thrown over a workbench. I guess my curiosity got the better of me, so I decided to take a look at what might be under it.

To say I was shocked would be an understatement. As I pulled the tarp back, there had to be thousands of dollars' worth of high tech radio equipment—and it looked pretty new. *What in the world would Martha have need for all this stuff?* I wondered. As I was putting the tarp back in place, I noticed a wire, probably an antenna, that went through a small hole in the back wall. I removed one of the fishing poles and went outside to see if the wire I had found went anywhere.

This was really strange. The wire, which someone would hardly notice, traveled up into a large tree, and where it terminated there appeared to be some type of dish array hidden by leaves that no one would ever see unless they really were looking for it. My imagination was getting the better of me again. *What would an eighty-year-old woman be doing with equipment like this?* I thought to myself.

There were more questions than answers, but I was just going to wait to see if Martha might bring up the conversation. I took the fishing rod and went back to the cabin to get the tackle box, and then headed to the rock outcropping I had been sitting on last night. It seemed as good a place as any to try my luck.

The events that had taken place still had my mind racing. Dad and Mom being mixed up with people that had some agenda, a cabin in the middle of nowhere with hi-tech radio equipment, and a man named Jack Hastings that worked with my parents and knew intimate details about them, let alone the call Jack had made last night to my mom. All extremely bizarre.

I would just have to let things play out. Sooner or later, I was sure I would find out what was going on and be able to fit all of these puzzle pieces together. For now though, it was time to catch my dinner.

40

As the day wore on, my luck at fishing had finally begun to pay off. I had landed two largemouth bass that had to be four pounds each. At least I knew what I would be eating this evening. As I sat on the rock casting my line, the thought had occurred to me that our country had so much open space for people to enjoy themselves. I had read somewhere that President Teddy Roosevelt often came out to these parts, and there was even a national park named after him somewhere west of where I was.

It had to be past noon when I decided to head back to the cabin with my catch-of-the-day. Once I got back, I found a pretty sharp knife and was able to clean the fish I had caught and cut four really nice fillets, which I salted and placed on a plate in the fridge.

Martha had left a bag of rolls and some assorted cold cuts in the fridge, so this was as good a time as any to have lunch. As I sat down to eat I was startled when I heard a loud screeching sound coming from across the lake. It sounded almost like a woman screaming. I got up from the table and opened the door to see if I could see anyone, but couldn't see a soul anywhere around. Then there was that screeching sound again.

I picked up a rock and flung it across a narrow portion of the lake. It ended up hitting a tree and then I saw it—an owl took off screeching its head off. Then I remembered from my old Boy Scout days that a certain kind of owl made a similar sound. I guess as a city boy I had to get acclimated to sounds I hadn't heard since I was a kid. But if you didn't know what that sound was coming from, you would have thought someone was getting murdered.

Having identified the mysterious sound, I returned to the cabin and finished my lunch. Once I cleaned up, I decided to take a walk around the lake just to get some exercise. I felt as if I had been sitting on busses or on hard seats in bus stations or eating-places for days, so I figured a walk would do me good and maybe clear my head while I waited for Jack to return.

The lake had to be a couple of miles long, so a four-mile walk around couldn't hurt. Back in Georgetown you could always find me on the soccer field—I just wasn't used to being this inactive. There was no question that the countryside was really a remarkable sight, with mile upon mile of vast open spaces. I could only imagine what the early settlers thought when they saw areas like this. The beauty of the place just took one's breath away.

I imagined it took a bit of getting used to for folks that traveled out here from a city, as it was deathly quiet, and no one around as far as the eye could see. As I approached one end of the lake, I saw it terminated at a small hill that I decided to climb. When I reached the top, I had a panoramic view of a vast valley, with a small river running through it. I only wished that I were not here under these circumstances—and a camera really would have come in handy at this point.

I walked back down the hill and continued on around the other side of the lake. I was almost back to the cabin when I heard something in the distance. I began to pick up my pace, and when the cabin was in sight, I saw Martha pulling up in her truck. Then I also could see that she had a passenger with her, but couldn't make out who it was.

As I got a little closer, I stood behind a tree and watched until the door from the passenger side opened, and out stepped Jack Hastings. All kinds of thoughts started racing through my mind. How did these two people even know each other? Martha then walked to the front door and opened it. Obviously I had forgotten to lock it before I had left for my walk.

I was close enough to overhear Martha say, "He's not here, Jack. He's probably down at the far end of the lake fishing. We can come back a little later."

Then Jack and Martha got back into the truck and headed out to wherever they had come from. I wasn't sure what I had just witnessed, but just maybe a few more puzzle pieces were coming together. Dad had made the original arrangements just in case something happened. Then when something did happen, I had found myself in North Dakota with an eighty-year-old woman and a guy that claims to know my parents. Considering that very expensive radio equipment I found in the back shed, there seemed to be more than meets the eye going on here, and somehow I knew I was going to have a part to play in this sinister scenario that kept unfolding, little by little.

41

Once Jack and Martha were out of sight, I returned to the cabin. Nothing was out of place, though I did want to check on the money my dad had left me. It was exactly where I had left it. At this point I had more questions than answers, and my only hope of finding out what was going on would be to confront Jack and Martha when they returned.

As much as I wanted to contact my friend, Paul, I thought it best to wait and ask Jack his opinion about it. The last thing I wanted to do was make a false move and jeopardize any plans that Jack might have been working on. How Martha figured in this was still an unsolved mystery for me, but I had no doubt that there had to be some reasonable explanation.

It was nearly three in the afternoon before I heard Martha's truck making its way back toward the cabin, and as I watched through the window, I saw she had brought Jack along with her again. I didn't want Martha or Jack to think I had spotted them earlier, so as I opened the front door to the cabin, I faked a surprised and confused look on my face.

"Martha? Jack? Do you two know each other?" I asked.

Martha looked at Jack as if to say, *You mean you didn't tell him?*

"Mike," Jack said, "let's go inside and have a talk."

We all walked into the cabin and Jack apologized for not letting me know that he and Martha actually had known each other for a very long time.

"Mike, I need to give you some background on what your parents, Martha, and I are all involved in. Did your dad ever mention to you anything about the Q *Group*? Or did you ever overhear a conversation where someone may have mentioned it?" Jack asked.

"To the best of my knowledge, Jack, this is the first time I ever heard the name. What's really going on here?"

"Mike, it's like this. Martha, your dad, and I—and also your mom—have been in the service of the Q Group for many years. Your dad and I have used this cabin as a kind of safe house for individuals we were entrusted to protect. The Q stands for *Quantum,* and the group is made up of hundreds of likeminded individuals that have been working tirelessly to keep our country safe."

"Jack, now you're losing me. What do you mean by keeping our country safe? Don't we have a military to do that? And state and local police?"

Jack looked at Martha and quipped, "I told you this wasn't going to be easy."

"Mike, I probably would have to give you the history of the world for the last four hundred years to explain all of this, but in a nutshell, this is all about control of the planet. Think of our world broken up into a four factions. Many times these different factions work at cross-purposes with each other, although on rare occasions they do cooperate. And a few times it has gotten very ugly."

"Jack, are we talking about world conquest here?" I asked.

"In a sense, yes, Mike. You see, these factions are controlled by some of the largest corporations in the world. Some control food and water, while others control the media, communications, transportation and banking."

"Jack, it sounds as if these factions you're describing have some pretty strong people behind them—and some big money."

"Mike, that would be putting it mildly, to say the least. These factions, who really can't stand each other, are very good at compartmentalizing information, so that literally the right hand never knows what the left hand is doing. They have well-placed agents all over the world, always watching events, and in some cases *creating* events, such as false flag incidents that can change the course of human history."

"Jack, what I don't understand is how you, Martha and my parents figure into all of this."

"Well, Mike, the Q Group is also backed by some very powerful people, who work tirelessly to free mankind from many of the oppressive tactics that these factions thrust upon society. For example, in our country one faction may send out agents to stir up trouble with race relations, while another faction is laundering drug-and-arms-sales money. Still another faction may have infiltrated the very halls of Congress, while they try to bribe some of its members. In a worst-case scenario, they may threaten a congressman with the death of a family member if he refuses to cooperate with their wishes. It's a pretty seedy side of our world that many people in the general public never learn about, and we're trying to change that."

"I had no idea this is how our world worked. It sounds like society is controlled by nothing more than rich bullies that want the world under their total control."

"Mike, now you are beginning to get the picture. And they're not only super-rich, but many of these people at the top are nothing more than psychopaths that could care less whether or not humanity survives."

"Okay, Jack, now I can better understand what this group is all about, but how do I figure into these plans?"

Martha had been sitting on one of the bunk beds twirling a ring of keys around her index finger while Jack talked. At this point Jack gave her a quizzical look, to which she responded: "Go ahead and tell him, Jack"

"Mike," Jack said, "when your mom and dad found out about the gift you had, they wanted to keep it as quiet as possible. Your dad trusted his friend, Dr. Stevenson, but that fool couldn't keep his mouth shut. Once the cat was out of the bag, Colonel Bridgewater is the type who would stop at nothing to get his hands on you and use you as an asset. Your parents had good reason to fear for your safety."

"Jack, does Bridgewater belong to one of these factions?" I asked.

"Yes, Mike, he does. And as I said, many of these agents like Bridgewater have already infiltrated our own government. The best your parents could do was to contact Martha and me to try to keep you safe for the time being, until we get further instructions."

"Guys, I never in a million years thought I would ever be caught up in something like this. It's going to take me a while to let this all sink in."

"Mike, that's totally understandable," Martha said. "Jack and I should be hearing from our counterparts soon, and then we will inform you of the next move. Okay?"

"I guess it will have to do for now, but is there any way I might be able to talk to Mom?"

"Mike, let's hold off on that for a day or so," Jack said, "just to make sure we haven't been compromised."

"Okay, Jack. I'm not going anywhere, that's for sure."

"Before I forget, Mike, here's your phone back. I retrofitted the electronics so that the phone is totally encrypted, and you'll also notice that red button I installed. If you ever believe your life is in any danger, just press that button—that's all you have to do."

At that point, both Jack and Martha made their way to the door, and just before Martha walked out, she turned and gave me a kiss on my cheek, as she said to me: "Don't you worry about a thing, Mike; we're going to take good care of you. Of that you can be assured."

"Oh darn, Martha, I almost forgot. I caught two largemouth bass, and I wanted to give you a couple of the fillets to take home. Hang on and I'll get them for you."

"Mike, my goodness, they are beauties! I'll get them right home and have them for dinner. Bless your heart, Dear."

42

To say I was floored by what I had just been told would be a gross understatement. Before running off from home I really should have had the presence of mind to bring along my laptop, or at least my own iPhone. On the other hand, a Wi-Fi connection using my own equipment probably would give away my location. There was just so much I wanted to learn and to read up on. I still had a million questions to ask Jack and Martha, but I would just have to wait until they returned.

The only thing I could do now was to take those two fish fillets and make dinner. After I fired up the stove and got it hot enough, I heated up a big iron skillet and got the fillets frying. Meanwhile, I took a look at the cell phone that Jack had altered, and was amazed at the knowledge that Jack and my father must have had to get them this far. I had no idea what was going to happen next.

Dinner was just about ready and I was starving. I plated the fish along with some macaroni salad Martha had purchased, and then grabbed a can of soda and went to town. The fish had a sweet taste to it, and the only thing lacking that I wish I had was a lemon to squeeze over it.

After I had finished, I just sat back in my chair and thought about the events that had transpired over the last twenty-four hours. My life had been turned inside out and upside down, but at least I knew my mother was in safe hands, and sooner or later I would be able to see her. I had no idea where she had been taken by the Q Group, and I just wished I could be in her company at the moment.

By the time I had cleaned up after dinner, it was just getting dusky outside, so I thought I might as well take a short walk before retiring for the evening—there really wasn't much else to do in the middle of nowhere. And other than Martha and Jack, there wasn't anyone to talk to.

The evenings did get cool in these parts, even in the summer months, so I put my jacket on before I headed out, and left the light on just in case I needed to find my way back in the dark. One other thing I decided to take with me was the modified phone that Jack had given me. I started walking in the direction of what became my favorite rock, when I heard a sound in the distance, but this time it wasn't a truck. I looked in several directions, but the echo of the sound I was hearing was bouncing all around and I couldn't make out the direction it was coming from. Then in the distance, I saw it. There was a helicopter flying at an altitude of around two thousand feet, but what scared me was the fact that there was a very strong light coming from the copter that was directed toward the ground—and it was getting closer.

As soon as I spotted the helicopter, I started running back to the cabin to kill the light I had left on. I made it just in time, and then just waited to see where the helicopter was heading. As it drew closer, my heart was literally in my mouth. I saw the helicopter's light bounce off the lake, and then it began to hover for a few breathtaking moments before finally continuing on its way.

At that point I didn't know why the helicopter was there, or what they were looking for, but the first thing that came to mind was to press that red button on the phone that Jack had given me. I waited a few more minutes to see if the helicopter returned, but the sound of its engine finally had faded into the night and never returned.

The one thing I knew was that the light from the helicopter never reached the cabin, and since I had shut the light off before it passed over, I figured they never saw the cabin itself. Then a disconcerting thought dawned on me: what if people in the helicopter had night vision equipment? Could they have seen the cabin without their light shining directly on it?

One other disturbing thing I noticed as the helicopter had come closer was that I could see someone inside the helicopter talking on his cell phone to someone else. I could hear part of his conversation while he was in my line of sight, but the constant movement of the helicopter made it difficult for me to stay focused, so I was able to catch only small snippets of what was being said, none of which made sense.

I was just beside myself, and finally decided to hit the red button on my phone. Within a couple of seconds Jack was on the other end.

"Jack, I don't know what just happened, but a helicopter just flew over the lake and it had a very bright light focused on the ground. I don't know what they were looking for, but it hovered over the lake for a moment, then flew off in a southeast direction."

"Mike, I'll get back to you in a couple of minutes. I want to check something out first. Just sit tight and I promise I'll get right back to you."

As I waited for Jack to call back, I looked out the window to see if I could see anything else out of the ordinary, but there was nothing to be seen. At this point I didn't know what was happening, but I had this strange feeling come over me that I just might have to move at a moment's notice. If I had to go on the run again, there wasn't all that much that I had to pack, but I wished that Jack or Martha would get back to me soon.

When the phone finally rang, I picked up on the first ring. "Hello, Jack. Glad you got back to me."

But the voice on the other end wasn't Jack's.

"Michael Brewer," the voice said, "we know where you are. It's time to stop running and surrender to us."

"Who is this?" I asked.

At that point the phone went dead. "Shit! C'mon, Jack. Call me back already!" I said out loud. Then I saw lights from a car or a truck heading my way, but the sound was unmistakable. It was Martha's truck. I had a funny feeling it was going to be time to go. So I grabbed all of my belongings and stuffed them into my backpack and then got up on the chair to pull down the bag of money my dad had given me.

Once the truck arrived, Jack jumped out and flung open the front door.

"Kid, you must have been reading my mind. Do you have that phone I modified?"

I handed the phone to Jack and he broke it in half and then flung it into the lake.

"Mike, we have to go, I'll explain on the ride out of here."

I got into the truck with Jack and Martha, and we took off like a bat out of hell.

"Jack, what in the world is going on?" I asked.

"Mike, I guess that phone wasn't as safe as your dad may have thought, and when you called your friend back home, the NSA must have discovered where you were. I must have gotten to that phone a little too late. Like I said, you can't imagine how good these people are. But no problem, Mike; we're going to be all right. Step on it, Martha. We have to make the rendezvous within the next thirty minutes."

"Don't you worry about me, Jack," Martha said. "This old girl will get you there."

43

To say that I felt like I was in a car chase scene out of a movie would not have described adequately the anxiety I felt at that moment. Martha was flooring the accelerator, and I was surprised at how much power her truck had, given its age.

"Martha," I asked, "just what kind of engine do you have under the hood of this thing?"

"Mike," Martha responded, "you wouldn't believe me if I told you. Jack and a few of his friends modified this old wreck just in case we had a situation like this come up. The engine is a 5-liter V-8. It pushes out 385 horsepower at 3,850 rpm's, and I'm nearing the red line now."

"Mike," Jack added, "that's not all this truck is equipped with. The outside of the truck may look rusted, but every square inch of the truck's cabin has been modified and is bullet proof, including the glass. And that's still not all."

"What else could you possibly have installed in this thing?" I queried.

"Well, Mike," Jack said, "you must have heard about the move to self-driving cars, right? Martha, show Mike what I mean."

At that moment Martha flipped a toggle switch and all of the truck's lights went out. Then Martha took her hands off the wheel while the truck was cruising along at ninety miles an hour.

"How in the world is this possible?" I asked.

"Mike, this technology has been around for a long time. It actually was created years ago, but was held back from the public until now," Jack said. "Our group has many technologies available to it when the need arises. What you're about to see once we get to our destination will blow your mind."

"Speaking of destinations, Jack, where in the world are we going?"

"Mike, we have a private airstrip we're heading to now; we'll be there in about twenty more minutes."

At that moment all of us in the truck saw a light shining down from the sky about a mile ahead of us. Jack told Martha to keep the lights off and then pull over to the side of the road until he felt it was safe to head out again. As we sat in the truck, Jack kept looking at his watch. The helicopter was making wider and wider circles as the light from it kept scouring the ground below.

Jack was getting really fidgety, and I could see he definitely was a nail biter. As we watched the helicopter getting closer, suddenly it veered off in a totally different direction. It was then that Jack told Martha to get going, and did we ever go!

"Mike," Jack said, "these mental cases will stop at nothing to get their hands on you. In fact you probably would be a crown jewel in their arsenal that is used against society. In the right hands, however, your ability could be utilized in a positive way, for good rather than evil, and your mom and dad knew that only too well."

"I totally understand, Jack, and now I have a pretty good idea that the life I thought I would have has all but evaporated. So I was wondering if it would be possible for me to become an agent of change for good in the world."

"We were kind of hoping you might feel that way, Mike," Jack said, as Martha smiled broadly.

At the rate Martha had been moving, we made it to our destination with several minutes to spare. We were in the middle of a field that had what looked like a roadway. But where, I wondered, would we go from here? Then Jack said, "Now we just wait."

There wasn't any sign of the helicopter, and both Jack and Martha seemed to have no doubt who they were looking for. We waited another five minutes and then off in the distance I saw what appeared to be a star. Only this star was getting brighter by the second.

"There's our ticket out of here, Mike," Jack said.

Then he turned to Martha and said, "The jet will be landing in another minute or so. You'd better hightail it out of here, Martha. As usual, you've been a great asset to the cause. I'll take care of Mike from here."

Martha gave me a big smile and a light pat on the cheek before she pulled away into the night. I grabbed all of my belongings and Jack and I walked over to a single large tree with a huge rock next to it. As we waited to get going on the next leg of this incredible journey, suddenly a very bright light appeared to hit the ground about one thousand feet away from us, which meant the helicopter was back. It was then that Jack pulled what looked like a satellite phone out of his jacket and told the plane to move away and try again in two hours.

The next thing that blew my mind happened when Jack pulled another device out of his pocket that looked like a small pager. After pressing a button, I couldn't believe what I was seeing. The top of that huge rock we were standing next to suddenly lifted up. It was totally artificial and hollow inside.

"Get in, Mike," Jack said.

We both took cover inside the rock and then Jack pressed another button and the top came back down. No one ever would have guessed that the rock wasn't real, much less that there was anyone hiding in it. By then the helicopter was hovering in the area, and there was no doubt that whoever was in it was looking for me. There were very small holes bored through the rock in order for the occupants to see out, and when Jack took a look outside, he told me to be absolutely quiet. I wondered why, and then, as I peered out one of the holes. I understood why.

44

The helicopter was hovering about five hundred feet away from us when I saw what appeared to be ropes dangling down from it, and then we saw several men in totally black clothing and black ski masks sliding down the ropes. We counted five men that came down from the copter, who then began fanning out looking at the ground. They were not using flashlights, but had these weird contraptions on their heads, and Jack whispered, "Night vision, Mike."

We watched as a couple of the men walked closer to the artificial rock we were hiding in. Then we heard one of them say, "They must have been here. There are fresh tire tracks in the grass. Better radio the chief and ask what he wants us to do."

One of the men began talking into a microphone that was attached to his outfit. When he had finished, he told the others to head back to the chopper and they would check out another quadrant.

"If I know their M.O., they're going to head back in the direction of the lake where they picked up the signal from your phone," Jack said.

We watched as all of the men that had come down began climbing the ropes back up to the helicopter, and once they were all in, the helicopter took off in the direction of the cabin, which was west of our position.

"We can get out of here now, Mike," Jack said. "I'm going to wait a few more minutes and then make contact with the jet. Our routine in a situation like this is just to have them circle for a while and then make a second attempt."

At least five minutes had passed and then Jack reached the pilots on the jet.

"You're clear for a second attempt," Jack said.

The voice on the other end said, "No can do, Jack. We know they're tracking us on radar. Head to the alternate pick-up point; we're heading back to base."

"Are we going to have to get on the run again?" I asked Jack.

"I'm afraid so, Mike. Knowing Martha, she's only about half way back to her place. I'm going to call her to come back to get us."

Jack grabbed his satellite phone and was talking to Martha in no time

"Martha, it's Jack. We're going to have to go with Plan B."

"No problem, Jack, I'll be there in a few. I'm only about eight miles from the drop-off location."

I turned to Jack and asked him where we would have to go next, and he answered, "Billings, Montana. Sorry, Mike. It's going to be about a five-hour drive. It's roughly 385 miles, but knowing Martha, we'll make it in record time."

"What happens once we get to Billings," I asked Jack.

"There's going to be a second attempt for a pick-up at another landing strip we use there. At least we know the chopper is heading west back to the site of the cabin, and we're going to be heading southwest to Billings, so I'm not expecting our friends to come back."

"I sure hope not, Jack. Does this happen all the time in these situations?" I asked.

"I've been in worse spots, Mike. The secret here is always to have a plan, and stay one step ahead of your enemy."

"Jack, I honestly can't believe all of the prep work and planning that must take place when getting involved in situations like this," I said.

"It does take a bit of work, Mike, but the payoff is always worth the time and trouble. Besides, I always get a kick out of screwing with the enemies' heads," Jack said, with a devious grin.

"Well, Jack, this is a whole new world for me. So far I have had a really simple life back home, like with friends I've known for years, and looking to a future as a microbiologist. Can I ask you a question?"

"Sure, Mike. Shoot."

"If the people from these factions are after me for my ability to spy on people and overhear phone conversations, what is it that the Quantum Group wants with me, other than the fact that my mom is involved with them?"

"Mike, I'm afraid that is way above my pay grade. But I can tell you this. You'll never have to worry about not being safe, where your next meal is coming from, or the amount of money you make per year. I think it would be pretty accurate to say that should you decide to work with us, you're going to have a life that you never imagined."

"Thanks, Jack. I know the life I planned is now nothing more than a faded dream. Nothing is ever going to be the same for me. Is there any chance that I might be working with Mom on some assignments?"

"Hard to tell, Mike. Let's first get you safely out of the country. By the way, your last stop is going to be Belize, and that's where your mother is."

"Oh wow, Jack. I will be so happy to see my mother again. And I've always wanted to visit Belize. You know their rain forests would be a microbiologist's dream."

"How so, Mike?" Jack asked.

"So, what a microbiologist does, Jack, is to study the world of organisms that are too small to be seen except with a microscope. I'll bet anything that there are plant species that could help eradicate some disease that afflicts mankind; already many cures have come out of the world's rain forests. At one time I even considered becoming a botanist, but decided that microbiology is what I really wanted to get into."

"Sounds like you had your life pretty well planned out, and I'm sure both of your parents were pretty supportive," Jack said.

"Jack, do you hear that?" I asked.

"I sure do, Mike. I would know the sound of that exhaust system a mile away, and that's about how far Martha is, and just in time. We have to make tracks now. Let's start walking and meet the old girl half way."

Jack and I didn't have to walk far, as Martha was roaring in our direction.

"You boys looking for a ride to Billings?" Martha asked, as she started laughing.

We both got into the truck and hit the road as fast as Martha could go to get us to Billings.

45

I couldn't figure out how an eighty-year-old woman could even keep her eyes open at this time of night, but I wasn't going to question that or the great good luck we had in ditching the helicopter. Martha looked at Jack and then asked, "Should I tell him?"

"That's up to you, young lady," Jack said.

At that moment, Martha asked Jack to take hold of the wheel for a second, which he did. I was then in for the shock of a life time when Martha took both hands and fumbled with something I thought was around her neck. With one sharp upward-lifting motion, Martha peeled off a full facial mask, and to my utter surprise, Martha wasn't some old lady at all. She couldn't have been more than forty years old!

"Are you freaking kidding me?" I exclaimed, in disbelief. "This cloak and dagger stuff only happens in the movies."

At that moment, Jack and Martha were laughing hysterically, and while we were on the road, both began telling me about some of their past exploits and some of the jams they had found themselves in. I thought to myself, *These people are at the top of their game, and I can only imagine what kind of world I'm now becoming a part of.*

As we kept driving, Martha remarked: "I know there's a small diner and gas station not too far up the road, Jack. You think it's safe enough to make a quick pit stop? I sure could use a cup of coffee, and I have to gas up if we're going to make it nonstop to Billings.

"Sure, Martha, but pull up to the place slowly with the running lights off. I just want to take a look around first."

In a couple of minutes we were at the place, and it looked as though they were getting ready to close. Jack got out of the truck and ran to the front door and motioned for whoever was inside to come to the door.

"We're just about on empty," Jack said to the man inside. "Can we just get some gas and then be on our way?"

The man motioned to Jack to pull the truck around to the pump. Jack waved Martha forward, and as soon as she got out of the truck, the lights on the pump lit up and she started filling the truck's gas tank. After she was done, since it didn't look like any of us were going to get coffee, Martha said she had bottles of water behind her seat and that would have to do.

Jack checked the pump, and when he saw it registered exactly $20, he pulled out a twenty and gave it to the man that had opened the door to the diner, and we were on our way to Billings.

"Shit, I really wanted that cup of coffee, Jack," Martha said.

"Stop your whining, girl. We'll find some other dive to take care of your caffeine cravings. Now step on it."

We were going to be traveling for several hours and I told Jack I just had to close my eyes for a while. Jack was sitting next to Martha and I was leaning against the passenger door. I wasn't one hundred percent sure how these people ever connected, and honestly, I wasn't sure if I wanted to know. I was just dog-tired and wanted to get some sleep.

It seemed that no sooner had I closed my eyes than Jack was shaking my shoulder, telling me to wake up. We had driven only a couple of hours, but Jack had received word from his contacts that there was a state police roadblock about five miles up ahead of us. Jack's contacts didn't believe the authorities were looking for us, but decided not to tempt fate.

Jack asked Martha to pull over for a minute while he checked out other routes to Billings. Martha said she knew a way around the roadblock, and that the detour wouldn't really add that much time to our trip. Jack told her to take whatever route she knew. We had to make time because the jet we were supposed to catch wasn't going to wait around long.

Martha hit the gas and after traveling for about a mile, she turned off onto a dirt road that had been well traveled. It wasn't long then until we came across another road that looked like it was in the middle of a cornfield. She turned the truck to the right, and we were on some backcountry road that was pitch black. The only roads with streetlights were in small towns that dotted the landscape.

Once Martha was certain we had avoided the roadblock, she got back on the main road that eventually would get us to Billings and out of harm's way. Meanwhile, Jack was always listening to a scanner that was in the truck for any sign that either the local police or anyone else was after us. Everything was quiet except for a few truckers that were going back and forth on their CB radios.

I asked Martha how much longer she thought the trip might take, and she said, "Maybe another couple of hours. Not that much longer."

"Great," I said. "I'm going to try again to get some sleep."

For all I knew, my two new friends could have been on amphetamines, because I had no idea how in the world they were keeping their eyes open.

46

I didn't know how far we had traveled, but I woke up when I felt the truck slowing down. I barely had my eyes open as I wondered what was going to happen next. Martha had stopped when she could see the lights from Billings several miles in the distance.

"We're not going to the Billings Airport, are we, Jack?" I asked.

"No, Mike, there's a private air strip about two miles ahead. I think it best we just wait here for some response from the jet, and then we'll make our move."

As we sat waiting for some word from the jet crew, I turned to Martha and asked her why she went through all the trouble putting on the old lady act?

"Well, Mike," Martha said, "we have several of these safe houses like the cabin you were staying at. When I originally bought the place about ten years ago, I knew that people in small towns seemed to know everyone, and I really didn't want to bring any attention to myself, as a newcomer. I knew that if I hit town as a young, single woman, I probably would attract too much attention from some of the younger cowboys in the area; and so with a bit of help from the Q-Group I aged myself to look like a nice old lady that just wanted to live on her own and not be bothered by the outside world. People around these parts know well enough to respect other people's privacy. It has worked out pretty well, I'd say. Then when I was contacted by Jack that we had a job to do, I flew out to Crosby from Washington DC, where I was stationed.

"Wow, Martha, you people must plan years in advance," I commented.

"In many cases we do, Mike. But in situations like this, even the best plans can go south pretty fast, so a lot of things have to be made up on the fly."

"I'm just amazed at how the two of you had this all figured out," I said.

"It gets easier over time, Mike."

Jack broke in, "But in your case we had to move pretty fast."

At that moment, Jack's phone came to life. It was the jet crew. They were ten miles out and would be doing a stop just long enough to pick us up, and they asked us to be ready.

"We'd better get going, Martha. We don't want to keep them waiting," Jack advised.

Martha started driving and within just a few minutes we were at the designated area where we were supposed to meet the incoming jet. There must have been a low cloud layer, because this time we couldn't see the incoming lights on the jet as we had seen before. Once the plane dropped below the clouds it made a sharp bank to the left and then turned on final approach to the landing site.

Jack checked the tail number to be sure it was the same number he had been given in a previous conversation with the crew. He just wanted to make sure that we had the right plane, from the right people. There were no do-overs in this incredible game of hide-and-seek.

Once the plane was on the ground, it taxied back to the spot where we were waiting, then came to a full stop but left the engines running. A door opened just behind the cockpit and a man in military fatigues walked down the short stairs to greet us.

"Hey. Jasper," Jack said, as the two shook hands. "Been a while, hasn't it?"

"Hey, Jack. How's it going? Oh hi, Martha, I didn't see you standing there. Is this the package?" Jasper asked Jack.

Package? Were they talking about me? I wondered.

"It sure is, Jasper, and you'd better take good care of it. There's someone very special waiting for him when you land," Jack replied.

"Okay, folks, let's get a move on," Jasper said. "Martha, you keep a warm spot in your heart for me, and maybe we can catch up with each other some time."

"Sure, Jasper. Keep dreaming," Martha said, as she let out a big laugh.

Martha turned to Jack and told him he'd better get on board. As I was walking toward the plane, Martha called me over to her.

"Mike, I know this has been very difficult for you, and perhaps the worst part was losing your dad. He was a great man and helped our group immeasurably in the past. I don't know what the future may hold for you, Mike. That's going to be a decision that will have to be made by you, along with the upper echelon of the Q Group. Just remember, Mike, that the gift you have is like none other. It can be used for good as well as evil, but I know you're smart enough to know the difference. And I know you're going to be in good hands. Now get on board and have a safe trip. I should be down to Belize in a couple of weeks, and by that time you should be pretty much settled in your new home-away-from-home."

"Martha, thank you so much for everything you've done for me, as well as my family. I'm not sure what my life may have in store for me, so I guess the best I can do is just take each day as it comes."

I then gave Martha a kiss on her cheek as I turned to get on the plane. When I reached the top of the stairs, I turned one more time and waved to her before entering the plane. Jack pulled up the door and latched it, and within another minute, we were ready to get airborne.

When I reached my seat, I waved to Martha once again as the jet began to turn toward the runway. Suddenly, the unexpected happened. One engine just shut down. Jack got out of his seat and asked Jasper what was going on.

"I'm not sure, Jack, but I think the main oil pump to one of the engines just quit."

Jack ran to open the door before Martha took off, and yelled, "Martha! Wait a minute!"

It didn't take Jasper long to determine that it would be too dangerous to fly with just the one engine. Jack got off the plane and was talking to Martha, probably about yet another change of plans.

What else could go wrong? I wondered.

After talking to Martha, Jack came back on board and asked me to grab my belongings. We were going to have to do this another way. I got off the plane and walked over to the truck and asked Martha what we were going to do now.

"Not to worry, Mike. We have backups to the backups."

47

After the three of us piled back into the truck, Jack dialed someone on his satellite phone.

"Billy, its Jack Hastings, and I need a favor."

I could hear the man on the other end saying in a semiconscious voice, "Do you know what time it is?"

"Who else do you think I'd call at this time of night if I needed a favor? I need a ride from Billings to Jackson Hole, Wyoming. Get your ass out of bed and we'll meet you at your hangar at Billings International in thirty minutes. Get moving now!"

After his call, Jack told Martha to head back to the turn-off and then get going to the airport in Billings. By now I definitely had a great appreciation for the quick thinking both Jack and Martha exhibited.

"Is Billy ready to go?" Martha asked Jack.

"Billy is always ready, unless he was drinking like a fish the day before."

"Jack, are you sure this guy Billy can be counted on?" I inquired.

"Don't worry, Mike. He's one of us, and the trip by plane won't take all that long. Maybe ninety minutes. I'm going to call home base and make sure the jet we had as a spare is ready to go the minute we land."

While Jack was making the final arrangements for the backup jet, Martha was being cautious to a fault as she began to enter Billings International airport. Given the current climate with terrorists, she probably wanted to make sure we didn't attract any undue attention.

After driving around a large traffic circle, Martha turned onto a service road on the side of the main terminal where private planes were parked. She pulled up to one of the hangars, killed the lights, shut the engine off, and then we just waited for Jack's associate to show up.

It didn't take long until a red Jeep pulled up behind us and the guy that got out nearly fell on his face as he stumbled over to the truck.

"Billy, my man, am I glad to see you," Jack said.

"I'll bet you are," he said in what could only be described as a very disgusted tone of voice. "Get your damned ass out of that truck and help me slide the hangar door open."

Jack got out of the truck and both men pushed the door open. Then Billy turned on a light and I could see his plane. I asked Martha if she knew what type of plane it was and she said it was a brand new Diamond Twin Star that accommodated three passengers plus a pilot, with a top cruising speed of 192 knots.

"Don't worry, Mike," Martha assured me. "You really are in good hands. Billy just gets a little grumpy when he's been awakened from a sound sleep, but he does get compensated very well for his time. I think this finally is going to be the end of the line for me. Let me check with Jack, and you just wait here in the truck.

Martha walked over to Jack and Billy, but I had this strange feeling come over me that something wasn't quite right. I couldn't hear what was being said, but I sensed that an argument had erupted. At that moment, Billy pulled out a pistol and pointed it at Jack and Martha. What the fuck was going on now?

Billy had Martha and Jack move over to a side of the hangar where there was a phone. At this point, I felt I had to do something, and saw my chance. I quietly got out of the truck and made my way into the hangar without this Billy-person seeing me. I wasn't more than ten feet from him when there, on some type of rolling workbench, I saw a large wrench. I knew I would never make it to the guy to hit him, but I could create a diversion. I threw the wrench over to the other side of the hangar, and as Billy turned to see where the noise came from Jack let him have it with one of the hardest blows I've ever seen a man throw.

Billy was out cold, then Jack asked Martha and me to close the hangar door. While we took care of the door, Jack picked up a roll of duct tape and bound Billy's hands behind him, and then bound his legs as well. Lastly he placed a piece of tape over Billy's mouth.

"Martha," Jack said, "Billy turned. Someone must have gotten to him and offered him a pretty good bounty for Mike. I can't believe this scumbag was bought off. Look, Martha, if we don't get out of here soon, we'll never get to make the hookup in Jackson Hole. You know what has to be done, don't you?"

"Yes, Jack, I do. Let's drag him to the back of the hanger."

I had no idea what was coming next.

I watched as Martha and Jack dragged Billy to a back corner of the hangar, and then Martha removed a pistol with a silencer from under her jacket. She never hesitated once, and put a single bullet into Billy's head. At that point I nearly tossed my cookies, but somehow managed to keep down what little food I had in me.

"Now what the hell are we going to do?" I asked Jack.

"Nothing has changed, Mike. Instead of three people on the plane, there will be only two, you and me."

"Jack, on top of everything else you do, do you mean to tell me you also can fly?" I asked,

"Just watch my smoke, Mike."

"Martha, I'm going to open the hangar door and Mike and I will push the plane out. Get in the truck and when you have the chance, give home base a call and tell them what happened, and that I'm on the way with the package."

"Good luck, Jack. Just make sure you get clearance from the tower before you take off, or they'll send a fighter jet after you," she joked.

"Not to worry, Martha. We've done this plenty of times and I know the drill. Mike, climb aboard, we're going for a ride. Martha, get your ass out of here. I'll make contact when we reach Jackson Hole."

Martha ran back to the truck and cranked it up, but sat there with the engine running as she watched to be sure we got off.

Jack entered the plane and did some checks, playing around with the instruments, and then started up the two engines. He radioed the tower asking for clearance and within a few minutes we were airborne.

48

Jack received clearance from the tower to taxi to the end of the runway. When clearance came for takeoff, Jack moved the plane into position in the middle of the runway, and pressed down on the brakes as he revved up the engines. When he released the breaks we rolled down the runway and were in the air in a matter of seconds.

"Jack, can I ask you a question?"

"Sure, Mike. Go ahead."

"How many people have you and Martha killed in your line of work?" I asked.

"Honestly, Mike, I've probably lost count. It's something that comes with the territory. This line of work, if you want to call it that, can get really messy at times. Unfortunately, Billy must have been offered a great deal of money to get rid of both Martha and me, and then to hand you over to Bridgewater's goons."

"You know, Jack, I've never seen a person killed before in real life. Of course I have watched it in movies, and honestly, I never thought it would affect me as it did. I realize you and Martha did what you felt you had to do, but why not just leave him there bound up? He wasn't going anywhere."

"Mike, Billy placed himself in that position, and if we had left him alive, he would have contacted the people that bought him off and we would have only more problems. My mission was to deliver you safely, alive, and in one piece, and that is exactly what I'm going to do, Mike. I owe that much to your parents."

"Jack, I can't believe I can keep my eyes open now. It's been one hell of a day."

"Mike, why don't you put the seat back and try to take a nap. We should be hitting Jackson Hole in about an hour and fifteen minutes; I can use some time alone myself, if you know what I mean."

"Sure, Jack. I could easily fall off in a New York minute."

As I drifted off, I knew the work that Martha and Jack did had to be stressful to the max. How I was going to fit into the grand scheme of things was probably the biggest question I had, but I knew once I was able to catch up with Mom, I probably would have some answers.

It seemed like only a matter of minutes after I had closed my eyes when Jack gave me a nudge and said we were twenty miles from our destination. I rubbed the sleep from my eyes and off in the distance I could see some lights.

"Is that Jackson Hole, Jack?" I asked.

"It sure is, Mike, and I already called ahead to the crew on the backup jet and they're ready to leave as soon as we touch down."

"How long do you think it will take to go from Jackson Hole down to Belize?"

"If I had to take a guess, somewhere in the neighborhood of five hours, Mike."

Jack then contacted the tower at Jackson Hole for landing instructions, and soon Jack was banking to turn north for landing. Just as he came out of the turn, I was able to see the runway lights.

Our landing was pretty smooth, and Jack asked me to look for a jet that had a particular registration number on its side. We passed a few planes and then I said to Jack, "I found it!"

"Right over there, Jack," I said, pointing. "That's the one."

Jack began to taxi the plane to an area that was designated for smaller aircraft, and as soon as he killed the engines, a black SUV pulled up next to our plane. Now I started getting worried. *Could the creeps have found us?* I wondered. Jack didn't seem worried, and then I understood why. He slid a window open and at the same time a blacked-out window on the SUV came down.

"Hey Jack, it's about time you got your act together."

"Monty, is that you, you old buzzard?"

"We were giving you up for lost. I heard about Billy from Martha, and by the way, you'd better give her the call you promised or she's going to kick your ass from here to New York."

"I know, Monty. Thanks for reminding me."

Jack and I got out of the plane and then Jack introduced me to the man he was talking to.

"Michael Brewer, I'd like to introduce you to Monty Lafarge. Monty was one of the original founders of the Quantum Group," Jack said.

"It's a pleasure meeting you, Mr. Lafarge. Did you know my dad or ever work with him?"

"Michael, your dad was one of the finest men I ever had the chance to meet, as well as work with. I was sincerely sorry to hear of his passing at the hands of Colonel Bridgewater's people. But we can talk about it on the trip down to Belize. I think we'd better get a move on."

The three of us got into the SUV and were driven a short distance away where we pulled up next to the jet I had spotted after we landed. I noticed the two pilots already in the cockpit, and we immediately walked up the stairs and into the main cabin. We all took a seat and buckled ourselves in. At that point the pilot stepped out and asked if we were ready. Monty simply told the pilot to get going.

As the engines on the jet began to rev up, I finally felt that in a relatively short period of time, I might be seeing Mom again. I knew there was a lot to catch up on, and I couldn't wait to see her.

49

After we were airborne, Monty turned to Jack and commented, "I can't believe that Billy would have sold out. He must have been offered a king's ransom for Michael."

"I know, Monty; it sure seems to be getting harder and harder to find good help these days"

"Seriously, Jack, did you take the proper precautions in covering your tracks?"

"Not to worry, Monty. Martha has taken care of everything."

"Michael," Monty said, "it sounds like you've had a few exciting days this past week. I'd like you to know that your father's death was not in vain, young man. With some help from your amazing gift, the Quantum Group hopefully will aid us in making things right, and our dear friend Colonel Bridgewater is going to pay a very high price for what he did."

"I appreciate that, Mr. Lafarge."

"Please call me Monty, Michael."

"This is all kind of new to me, as I had no clue about what my own parents were involved in. Jack has given me some idea as to what the Quantum Group is all about, but I'm sure there will be much more to discuss. Right now,

Monty, my thoughts are pretty scattered, and I really would like to just close my eyes for a while, if it's all right with you and Jack."

"Of course, Michael. I fully understand, considering what you have gone through over the last few days. There's a bedroom at the rear of the cabin. By all means, Michael, make yourself comfortable, and if there is anything you need, just let us know. Otherwise, you'd better get some rest. I know you can't wait to get together again with your mother."

"Thank you, Monty. I'll see you guys a little later."

"Catch a few Z's for me, Mike. See you later."

I excused myself from Monty and Jack and made my way to the back of the cabin. This wasn't some little Lear jet. It had to be at least a McDonnell Douglas MD-90. This jet was equipped with all types of electronic gear, a lounge and dining area, a conference room, as well as the bedroom, which wasn't too shabby. I kicked off my shoes and removed my jacket. All I wanted to do was close my eyes, and as soon as my head hit the pillow, I was out like a light.

I really must have been tired because the next thing I heard was Jack knocking at the door to my cabin. I looked at my watch and realized I had slept for three hours.

"Mike, time to get up and have something to eat. Monty and I will meet you in the dining area."

"Okay Jack, I'll be out in a minute."

I put my sneakers back on and went into the bathroom just to throw some cold water on my face, and then made my way to the dining area.

"Good morning, Michael," Monty said. "Please have a seat and join us for breakfast. Do you feel a little better after getting some sleep?"

"Yes, Monty, it was much needed."

One of the pilots, Peter, came to the dining area and asked all of us what we might like to have for breakfast?

"Pete," Monty said, "why don't you bring us the works. I think we could pick and choose. No need to fuss over us."

"Very good, Mr. Lafarge."

It didn't take long for Peter to come back to us with two baskets of warm croissants, a platter of scrambled eggs, a large plate of crisp bacon, a basket of fresh fruit, coffee, and every type of jam possible. This was really a feast for the eyes. While we were having breakfast, Monty asked what I had planned doing with my life now that I literally had a target on my back.

Honestly, I don't know, Monty. One day I was studying to become a microbiologist and the next, my entire world was turned upside down and inside out. The first thing I'd like to do is get together with my mother and try healing from the emotional trauma of losing my dad."

"That's totally understandable and quite admirable, Michael. Your mother has gone through a great deal as well, and luckily we were able to extract her when we did before Bridgewater got his hands on her. Tell you what, Mike, we'll get you together with your mother and give you the time you need to decompress from all you have gone through. When you feel up to it, I would like to introduce you to some of the members of the Quantum Group, and perhaps you might have some spark of interest in what we do. You might even consider joining us, as you know the ability you have could greatly help us stop some of the madness that Bridgewater and his people keep perpetrating on society. It's just something to think about, Mike, and I never want you to feel that you're being pressured into our service."

"I really appreciate that, Monty. If you and Jack don't mind, I'd just like to go back to the cabin and get cleaned up before I see my mother again."

"Hey, Mike," Jack said, "you don't have to worry about us. We should be landing in about thirty minutes and I can use the time to brief Monty on what went on in the last forty eight hours."

"Thanks, Jack. I'll be back in a little while."

I was stuffed from breakfast and headed back to the bedroom. I got my belongings together and took a seat in a very comfortable leather chair in the corner of the room. Thoughts of my dad and better days came flooding back. I remembered I never did get back to Paul, and I really wanted to know how the soccer team made out with the final game of the season.

I wasn't sure what direction my life was going to take, or exactly what the Quantum Group was all about, but I figured once I had the chance to get back together with Mom, a lot of my questions would eventually get answered.

I felt the plane start losing altitude, so I knew we were getting close to landing. I gathered my belongings and made my way to the front of the cabin and took a seat with Monty and Jack as we prepared to land. I wasn't sure what was going to happen next, but at least I knew I would be getting together with Mom, and that was something I was very much looking forward to.

50

As the plane began to drop through the clouds, I could see the coastline of Belize not far off in the distance, along with several of its small islands. The ocean below seemed so soothing to my eyes as I gazed into the azure blue waters. I also could make out the white sales on boats as they caught the warm Gulf winds pushing them forward.

There was much to consider as I drew closer to my destination. So many questions and so few answers, but I knew in time the answers would come. Who were these people that my parents had kept me so insulated from? I wondered for a brief moment if I even knew who my parents were, as they had never made mention of this secretive life they apparently led.

We were low enough now to see the runway ahead, and I asked Monty how far was the drive from the airport to our final destination.

"Michael, once we land, there's a car, a white Land Rover, waiting for us, and it'll take us about 30 minutes to reach the villa," Monty said.

"Monty, it sounds like this place is actually in the jungle, right?" I asked.

"Mike, you're going to be in for a bit of a surprise when we finally reach the place, but I won't give it away," Jack added, smiling.

I wondered what type of surprise Monty and Jack had in store, but I was their guest and didn't push for any further answers. As the plane touched down on the runway my heart grew lighter at the prospect of seeing Mom again after my life had decided to take a drastic turn in such a different direction.

Just before we reached the end of the runway, the plane turned off and taxied toward what appeared to be an isolated part of the airport. When we came to a complete stop, Peter, the co-pilot, entered the cabin and told Monty that all arrangements had been made, and that our transportation was waiting just outside.

We unfastened our seat belts and began walking to the doorway. Jack told us just to wait a moment until a large metal staircase was moved into position in order for us to disembark from the plane. Monty walked down first, followed by Jack, and then as I came down I noticed a gentlemen standing by the Land Rover who had opened the doors for us. After we all piled in, Monty introduced the driver as Xavier Williston.

"Xavier, Michael is not only our driver, but also is the head of security from the grounds of the villa," Monty chimed in. "If there is anything you ever require, he will be totally at your disposal."

I actually was beginning to feel like royalty, having people at my beck and call, but honestly I had only one thing on my mind, and that was catching up with Mom. Xavier drove the Land Rover out of Belize City as we headed northwest on the Phillip Goldson Highway, which was nothing like the interstates we had back home. This road was roughly 95 miles long and terminated at the Mexican border.

We must have traveled about 15 miles before Xavier turned off onto a red clay-colored road, which looked as though it was leading to nowhere. Thick brush lined the road on either side, and then we began a steep climb as the Land Rover plowed ahead. Our elevation had definitely increased, and I honestly believed we were in the middle of nowhere.

After driving a few more miles, Xavier said we were almost there. Where, I wondered, was *there*, as I saw literally nothing but heavy tropical growth everywhere I looked. Then without warning, the jungle canopy opened into a small field where there stood a very small house, literally just a hut with a thatched roof made of palm fronds.

Monty then asked Xavier to pull up a few more feet and then stop.

"Is this the villa you were talking about, Jack?" I asked.

Jack and Monty looked at me and smiled, and Jack told me we were just going to wait in the car for a moment. It was then that Monty picked up a phone in the car and said, "We're in position."

At this point I had no idea what to expect next. In a matter of seconds, the ground began to give way, and it felt as if the car was sinking in quicksand.

"What in the world is happening?" I asked Jack.

"Mike, this is where the real fun begins," Jack replied, as a huge smile spread across his face.

I couldn't believe what was happening as the four of us in the Land Rover began to descend beneath the ground. Once the top of the car passed below ground level, another door slid over to enclose us, but rather than being immersed in total darkness, there were lights built into the walls of what seemed to be some underground elevator shaft.

"Jack," I exclaimed, "this is freaking amazing! It must have cost some big bucks to build something like this."

"Mike, it's just one of several places we use around the world for our operations. Hold on a minute, you haven't seen anything yet."

As the trip down continued, I asked Monty just how far down we would be going.

"When we hit bottom, Michael, we'll be roughly two hundred feet beneath the surface. Next we'll ride about a half-mile through a cave whose lake bed probably dried up millions of years ago, then we're almost home. This whole area is honeycombed with similar caves."

"This is really amazing, Monty. It must have cost millions to excavate something like this. I mean, this is like something straight out of a James Bond movie!"

Monty and Jack started laughing, and then Jack said we could thank the very people who thought they controlled the world for providing the funding for the place.

"We just love screwing with their heads," Jack added, with a big grin.

We finally reached the bottom of the shaft, and after Xavier drove us for a short distance, he stopped to let us out and said he was going to take the Rover to the garage and get it washed.

I looked at Jack and asked, "You also have a garage down here?"

"That's not the half of it, Mike," Jack said as he gave me a wink.

51

After we got out of the Rover, Xavier took off to parts unknown. I looked around, but all I could see was solid rock in any direction I looked. Then Monty, who was carrying a black walking cane with what appeared to be a gold ram's head on top of it, tapped a spot on the rock façade. At that moment the rock wall began to slide to the left, revealing a very large, stainless steel door that looked like a massive bank vault that was split in two, vertically. Monty then walked to a panel mounted on the wall next to the door, and looked into a device that scanned his right eye, and then a computerized woman's voice was heard to say, "Please enter your key code."

On the other side of the panel was some sort of keypad, where Monty entered his own secret code. I had seen a lot of Sci-Fi movies in my time, but never imagined anything like this existed in the real world. Then, as Monty stood back, the massive door began to open. The three of us then proceeded to enter what appeared to be a waiting area, where a gentleman in some type of security uniform was sitting at a semi-circular desk with a built-in computer screen, apparently equipped with some type of scanner unlike anything I had seen before.

"Welcome back, Mr. Lafarge. You too, Jack," the guard said. "I see you brought company."

"William," Monty replied, "I'd like to introduce you to Mr. Michael Brewer. He'll be our guest here, so please take good care of him."

At that point Monty placed his hand on the scanner, and then Jack did the same. After a couple of seconds, William gave both men a security badge to wear. William then asked me to place my hand on the scanner and issued me a security badge as well. After we all had received our badges, I noticed they appeared to have small chips in them like the newer credit cards that were coming out to the public.

"Mike," Jack said, "This badge is only temporary. Once you've been taken to the lab a little later, we'll get you permanently into the system."

"The lab?" I queried, as I looked at Jack.

"Don't worry about it, Mike," Jack said. "It's part of the identification process. The Quantum Group doesn't take any chances."

We then began walking through one of several tunnels. I noticed large glass walls, and behind some were rows and rows of different plants being grown, while in other rooms there were banks of large computers that were being watched over by several people in white coats. All kinds of thoughts were racing through my mind, but my ultimate goal at this point still was just to see my mother.

After walking a little further, Monty told Jack to take the corridor to the right so he could get cleaned up as well as debriefed, and then Monty turned to me and said, "Michael, are you ready to meet your mother?"

"Monty, I was wondering when that was going to happen. This is just an incredible place," I said. "I've never seen anything like it."

"In time you will see the rest of the place, Mike," Monty said. "But for now, just come this way."

After walking past several different hallways, we came to a set of doors that we walked through, and honestly, I thought I was standing in the *Garden of Eden.* There was Mom, cutting what looked like beautiful orchids, which she was gathering to place in a vase. She turned and looked at me in stunned silence, then blurted out:

"Michael, my God, I am so glad to see you. I have been so afraid I was going to lose you forever, like your father."

"Mom, I can't tell you how long I have waited for this moment!"

"Lois," Monty said, "I think I'll leave the two of you to catch up. I have several matters to attend to. Take all the time you need. The board members can wait before we introduce Michael to them."

After giving Mom the biggest hug ever, I turned to Monty and thanked him for everything that he had done in protecting Mom, and told him I was looking forward to meeting with anyone he would like a little later. Monty then smiled, turned, and left us alone in the room.

As we embraced each other, seeking comfort in the loss of a father and a husband, we both had tears in our eyes.

"Mom, I was so sorry to hear about what happened to Dad—I was just devastated when I heard the news. Why didn't you and Dad ever take me into your confidence to let me know about this other life you both were leading?"

With a rather serious face, Mom asked me to take a seat at a large work bench in what appeared to be a very large underground greenhouse, with some form of fiber optic lighting that must have come from somewhere outside the facility.

"Mike, I'm not sure how much Monty and Jack may have told you, but your father and I have worked with this group for over twenty years. We were called into service because of our work contacts, providing us with clearance to work within the military at the Pentagon. We never wanted you to know this for a number of reasons, the foremost of which was to protect you, Michael. Had anything ever happened to your dad and me, plausible deniability on your part would have protected you. The second reason was that we were sworn to secrecy, but now you will be filled in once you meet the board members of the Quantum Group."

"I just can't comprehend all of this, Mom," I said.

"Mike, in time you will come to understand that what the general public thinks goes on in our world is nothing more than smoke and mirrors. They think that life consists of going to work, paying their bills, and living from paycheck to paycheck. The world is far more complicated than that. But now, as much as I miss your father, at least I feel so much better knowing I haven't lost you as well, and I'm so thankful to Jack and Martha and Monty for all they have done. I know you must be tired after the last few days, so before we get into anything else, let me show you to your suite.

Mom put aside the flowers she had picked, and we left the greenhouse area and walked through several tunnels that then branched off in different directions.

"Mom, just how big is this place?" I asked.

"Mike, what you've seen so far is nothing. There are several levels below us."

"This is just mind-blowing, Mom," I said.

"Mike, notice the different colored lines on the floor. Should you ever get lost, simply follow the green line, and it will always bring you back to the living quarters; and just remember always to wear your security badge.

"Here we are, Mike; this is your suite, number 107. Mine is just a few feet away at 110. Why don't you take some time to get cleaned up and then get some rest. Your closets are full of clothes in your size and every amenity you could think of is at your disposal. Should you need anything, simply press the yellow button on the wall, and Xavier will cater to your every whim."

"Mom, I don't know what to say, but I'm beyond happy in knowing that we're together again. All of this is going to take a bit of getting used to."

"It took your dad and me a while to get used to this as well, but we had the advantage of seeing the plans for this place before it was ever built. Actually, there are several facilities just like this in different parts of the world. Take your time now to relax, and I'll come and get you in a few hours. I love you so much, Michael, but now we have to think about the future. I'll see you a little later."

After Mom left my room, the first thing I did was just sit down and try to take all of this in. My room was enormous, and one of the things I wanted to do was to check out my new clothes. I opened the closet door and was dumbfounded when I saw suits, shoes, jackets, socks, underwear—you name it, and it was there, including my favorite brand of blue jeans and some pretty cool sneakers in my exact size.

The bathroom was spacious, and the next thing I wanted to do was take a shower and then get some sleep. I could always try on some of the new clothes when I got up.

52

I must have been sleeping for several hours when I heard the sound of a tone, and then a voice telling me it was time to get up. I guess this was the Quantum Group's style of a wake-up call. I walked into the closet and picked out a pair of jeans along with a dress shirt, and a pair of socks and sneakers. After I got dressed, I just waited for whatever was going to take place next.

It didn't take long to find out. The next thing I heard was the sound of a doorbell, and when I walked over and opened the door, Jack was standing there with a big smile on his face.

"You ready to meet some people, Mike?"

"Sure, Jack. I hope I'm dressed for the occasion."

"You look great, Mike; we're not going to a fashion show. Come with me, because we have to get to another level of the facility."

Jack and I walked through a number of different corridors until we reached an elevator. As we stepped in, Jack hit a button that read *Conference Room* on the display.

"Mike, I think you'll finally get all the answers you've been looking for."

After the elevator came to a stop, the door opened to a huge domed room that had a massive circular conference table. The lighting was fairly dim and on the walls were eight massive TV screens, each with a very large image of a different part of the world, like you would see flattened out in history books. Major cities on the map were lit up in red, and there were several cities, such as Belize City, that were lit up in green. Other places had lights blinking. As I tried to take all this in, Mom entered the conference room and sat next to Jack and me. The last one to enter the room was Monty, who took a seat at the head of the conference table.

Monty had some type of instrument panel with a lot of buttons on it, but before we got started, he had a few words to say.

"Michael Brewer, I would like to formerly welcome you to the main operating headquarters of the Quantum Group. And now I'd like to give you some background on why the Quantum Group was established, what we have accomplished, and what the ultimate goal of the group actually is."

At this point, Monty hit a toggle switch and the lights in the room began to dim even further.

"Michael, the Quantum Group was established over twenty years ago by like-minded people from around the world, who saw the danger associated with other groups whose plan was to globalize not only the world's economies, but to gain the upper hand in controlling everything, from the production of food to the availability of the planet's fresh water and energy resources."

As Monty continued speaking, the large screens behind him displayed images of everything from waterfalls to fields of corn and other crops as far as the eye could see. There were also images of labs, like the one I had seen earlier, growing many different types of food products.

"The Group itself," Monty continued, "consists of a board of directors, who are some of the richest people on earth that have given freely of their resources, both financial and tactical. This has enabled us to thwart attempts by some of the most notorious factions on the planet who could care less whether humanity survives or not. People like Jack, Martha, your mother, and many others around the world are the Group's foot soldiers, who place their lives on the line every single day. However, our most important asset is our ability to gather intelligence, so that we may continue to stay one step ahead of those who would do the world harm."

As Monty kept talking, I began to realize that with my new ability, if I chose, I could be playing a significant part in this organization. Monty went on to say that the group had people strategically placed in venues such as banking, government, the world's markets, as well as in deep cover positions, all working as one coherent body.

"Michael Brewer," Monty said, "please allow me to introduce you to four of our board members. First though, I must apologize to you, because you will not be allowed to see their faces or to know their actual names. You will be allowed only to hear their voices."

The large television screen on the wall came to life, but each individual appearing on the screen could be seen only in silhouette.

"Good day to you, Michael; you may refer to me as *Entity One*."

"Hello, Entity One," I said.

"Good day to you, Michael, you may refer to me as *Entity Two*."

"Hello, Entity Two," I replied."

"Greetings, Michael. My name is *Entity Three*."

"Hello, Entity Three," I answered.

Then the last individual identified himself. "Welcome to our group, Michael. My name is *Entity Four*."

Entity One then began to speak.

"Michael, I think I can speak for all of us when we say that we are pleased that you have arrived safely. Mr. Lafarge has provided you with a cursory background on the Quantum Group, and it is our intent, through various covert deeds and actions, to bring our world back into alignment."

"May I speak, Entity One?"

"By all means, Michael."

"For the vast majority of my life, as an only child, I have lived a relatively simple life. Both of my parents not only have showered me with their love, but they also have exposed me to many wonderful events that have made me the man I am today. I was deeply saddened to learn of my father's death at the hands of those you work against, but after talking to my mother, as well as Mr. Lafarge, I now have a better understanding as to my potential place in an ever-changing world."

"That is quite admirable, Michael," Entity One answered. "Given the fact that your life has now dramatically changed, while realizing that people like Bridgewater will never give up trying to locate you, do you see any roll for yourself in our organization?"

"Entity One, that is a question I regret I cannot answer at this very moment. What I ask is only that you afford me additional time to understand what small part I may play in the Quantum Group's ultimate game plan."

"Michael" Entity One responded, "shortly you will be fully enlightened at a far deeper level, and also given greater insight as to how all of us, and thereby the free world, can benefit from the gift you possess."

"Thank you, Entity One, and the rest of you, for understanding my current state of mind, and I sincerely appreciate your considering me as an asset to the Quantum Group."

"My fellow board members," Entity Three said, "I believe we have completed everything on our agenda except for the test. Mr. Lafarge, will you proceed."

Monty arose from the conference table and signaled Jack to take his phone and leave the room, which he did. Monty then proceeded to walk to a far end of the conference room where it would have been impossible for me to hear him. He then made a call, which lasted all of twenty seconds. Monty then returned to his seat and Jack came back into the conference room.

"Michael," this is Entity Two speaking. "Can you tell us what Mr. Lafarge said to Jack?"

"No, I can't, Entity Two. Because it wasn't Jack that Monty called. It was Xavier. He gave Xavier a series of numbers that I can clearly recall. The number was 3.1415926, which is the formula for *Pi*."

"Michael," Entity Four said, "that is truly a spectacular gift you have, and I am in total amazement. Fellow members, I believe we have seen enough. When Michael feels up to it, I would suggest further testing at a greater distances, along with a complete medical evaluation. After that is completed, let us meet again, and perhaps by that time Michael may have come closer to a decision as to what path he may wish to follow. I will now adjourn the meeting."

At that point all of the screens went black and Monty joined the rest of us and said, "Dinner is served. Please, all of you join me."

EPILOGUE

Several weeks had passed and I had been given virtually free access to the facility. I also was allowed to go topside for short periods with an escort, usually Jack, Mom or Xavier. I knew that the life I had dreamed of was only that, a dream. After my initial meeting with the board members, my abilities were tested again and again, and in all cases I had passed with flying colors.

After Mom had taken me through the facility, I realized that there had to be at least seventy five to one hundred people who worked there at various times. I had met scientists working on everything from new forms of food production to advanced body armor, and I had met people that constantly monitored the movement of money around the world. It was the movement of those funds from various places that tipped off the Quantum Group as to a particular move of any of the factions.

For some reason I didn't fully understand yet why the Group also closely monitored the activities of several countries in regard to their space exploration programs. They also kept an eye on various UFO reports coming from countries such as the U.S., Mexico, England and China.

This was going to be a brave new world for me, and I was getting closer to making my final decision as to how I just might fit in. One of my deciding factors was the close proximity to my mother, realizing that neither she nor I could ever return home. Of greatest concern to me was that if I did accept the Group's offer, it had already been suggested that my appearance could be changed through advances in plastic surgery. There was a fully functioning hospital in the facility, as well as highly qualified surgeons that could be flown in at a moment's notice to radically change my appearance.

I felt that the old Michael Brewer was gradually fading into a distant memory. Did I miss my friends back home? Of course I did. But there was the real feeling that for whatever the reason, I was chosen for a greater purpose in life, and that eventually, in some measurable way, I could help to change the world for the better with this uncanny gift I had acquired totally by accident.

Yes, the world was rapidly changing and as time passed I began to understand that with poorly utilized resources, so many people would continue either to starve or be displaced by unnecessary wars. How often I had wondered what it might be like to be a fly on the wall in the Oval office or perhaps 10 Downing Street! Could my ability actually help to short-circuit someone's crazy plan that might have the potential to change the course of human history?

For some unexplained reason I would at times think about my failures as well as successes in life. Most of the time, failure and missed opportunity have the same root cause, otherwise known as apathy, and in many cases the world turned out to be different from what you had thought it was. Man always has seemed to find different ways to exterminate himself, and perhaps at some point he actually will, or at least come close to doing so.

If my gift could prevent just one catastrophic event, I realized I could look back at my life knowing that it did serve a purpose, one that had served humanity and the memory of my father. Soon my decision would be made. Perhaps it already had.

*****

"The only constant is change, continuing change, inevitable change; it is the dominant factor in society today. No sensible decision can be made any longer without taking into account not only the world as it is, but the world as it will be."

— *Isaac Asimov*

Made in the USA
Middletown, DE
27 December 2016